"I … wa… actually his ide… woman, the kind of woman he wanted to both protect from harm and push up against a wall and make scream with pleasure. But telling her that would be completely unprofessional. He was still on a job. "You're a beautiful woman."

She sighed again. "I don't feel beautiful. I feel foolish. And a little airsick."

"Here. Lie down and close your eyes." Hunter patted his legs, indicating she should stretch out.

He was attracted to her, yes, but he also felt... interest. That tug of desire, in both his groin and his chest. Not good. Not good at all.

Which made offering for her to sprawl across his lap incredibly stupid.

She glanced up at him with big brown eyes. "You're very hard."

"Excuse me?" He was working on it, but not there yet. If she kept shifting around like that, he would be, though, and she would get an earful.

"Your legs. They're very muscular. Not the best pillow."

Right.

She smiled up at him. "But thank you. I appreciate it." Squeezing his knee she added, "You're very sweet."

Now, that was a word no one had ever used to describe him.

And with that, his job got a whole hell of a lot harder.

Dear Reader,

As a Northern girl, my favorite thing to do in the winter is to escape it. Unlike those who revel in skiing and ice-skating, I spend the winter running from building to car to my house wearing seven layers of fleece. Aside from not moving because of family, I swear half the reason I continue to live in the North is for the excuse to head to Mexico every chance I get!

So my heroine, Melanie's, desire to experience the triple play of sun, sand and sexy times was easy to channel. While I've never had a hot bodyguard like Hunter accompany me on vacation, I did once lose sleep in Cancún due to a couple of amorous dolphins right outside my room. Sometimes truth is stranger—or funnier—than fiction!

I hope you'll enjoy this final installment of my From Every Angle trilogy with an unlikely pair forced together and finding love.

Happy reading,

Erin McCarthy

New York Times Bestselling Author

Erin McCarthy

Deep Focus

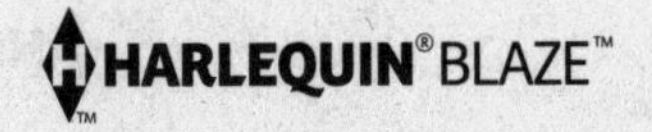

ISBN-13: 978-0-373-79846-9

Deep Focus

This edition published by arrangement with Harlequin Books S.A.

For questions and comments about the quality of this book, please contact us at CustomerService@Harlequin.com.

Printed in U.S.A.

USA TODAY and *New York Times* bestselling author **Erin McCarthy** was first published in 2002 and has since written over fifty novels and novellas in teen fiction, new adult and adult romance. Erin is a RITA® Award finalist and the recipient of an ALA Quick Picks for Reluctant Young Adult Readers Award. When she's not writing she can be found sipping martinis in high heels or eating ice cream in fleece pajamas depending on the day, and managing the lives of her two teens, two cats and her codependent dog. You can find Erin online at erinmccarthy.net or follow her on Twitter: @authorerin.

Books by Erin McCarthy

HARLEQUIN BLAZE

From Every Angle

Double Exposure

Close Up

COSMOPOLITAN RED-HOT READS FROM HARLEQUIN

Perfect 10

To get the inside scoop on Harlequin Blaze and its talented writers, be sure to check out blazeauthors.com.

All backlist available in ebook format.

Visit the Author Profile page at Harlequin.com for more titles.

Muchas gracias to Celso, Danny, Gil and Cuauhtemoc and the other guys at Fly High Adventures for always making my zip-line excursions and pit stops at the Three Amigos in Cozumel a blast.

1

SOMETHING WAS WRONG. Nearly everyone in the airport was naked.

Melanie Ambrose glanced around and frowned before rounding on her boyfriend. Dang it, he had broken their deal. "You said you were done working! We're on vacation, Ian, as of midnight last night. Our flight to Mexico is in an hour." She flung a finger out to point at the group of men and women sitting bare-assed on the hard plastic chairs in O'Hare's Concourse B. "This looks like work."

She shouldn't have trusted him to get to the airport on his own. She should have swung by his apartment and scooped him up, but it was out of the way and Ian hadn't wanted to stay at her place because he hated her bed. She'd agreed to arriving separate and now this. So annoying. Absolutely and utterly annoying. The whole reason their relationship was crumbling was because Ian worked all the time. She understood that his photography business was commercially successful beyond his wildest dreams, and that there were responsibilities and expectations, but this vacation was supposed to give him a much-needed rest. And her, a much-needed orgasm.

He held up his hands and gave her an apologetic shrug. "Mel, baby, I couldn't resist. I've not shot at the airport before, and what a perfect opportunity to capture the shuffling of humanity. It's brilliant. And I owe the idea to you."

She was not falling for that, or for his sexy New Zealand accent. "Whatever." She let go of the handle of her carry-on and looked down at her toes. The fifty dollars she'd just spent on a pedicure better not have been wasted. "We're not missing our flight," she told him flatly.

"Don't be so churlish," he reprimanded, pushing his glasses up. He looked past her, flagging someone down.

She turned and noticed one man in a suit, looking absolutely out of place amongst all this exposed flesh. The poor guy was probably just trying to catch a business flight and had wandered into Art. In the form of breasts and butt cheeks.

Melanie turned her attention back to Ian, giving him a glare. "It's nine in the morning! Our flight is supposed to leave at ten." She considered herself incredibly reasonable. She never complained about his schedule or questioned him about the company he kept. She respected his art, and as the PR rep for his company, Bainbridge Studios, she worked hard to make sure his climb up the ladder of success was smooth. But they'd been planning this trip for two months.

Escaping Chicago in December for the beach was bliss enough, but she'd been looking forward to the opportunity to rekindle a bit of romance.

Apparently, he wasn't in as much of a rush to drink

wine and knock boots as she was. It was a bit deflating. A lot deflating.

"I'll find a later flight. You go ahead as planned. Hunter will go with you."

Um. "Who the heck is Hunter?" Melanie's Southern accent was resurfacing as she became agitated. "And why on God's green earth would I want to fly to Mexico with him?"

"This is Hunter." Ian gestured behind her. "He's your new bodyguard."

Melanie turned and saw the man in the suit standing a discreet distance behind them. He nodded briefly. She was officially confused.

"Ian, why do I need a bodyguard? You're the one being stalked." Some woman who had never even met Ian fancied herself in love with him and had been bothering him for over a year. At one point, Savannah the Stalker had been charged and Melanie had thought that would be the end of it, but a jury had found her not guilty and almost immediately she'd gone back to sending alternating love letters and threatening emails. "She doesn't even know about us. That's part of why we've kept our relationship on the down low."

Another source of friction between them. It sucked having to pretend you were primarily your boyfriend's employee in public. She was over it.

Looking uncomfortable, Ian bent closer to her. "It seems she's found out about you, because I got a disturbing email a few days ago. I didn't want to tell you and spoil the trip. But I don't think it's safe for you to be without some protection."

Great. She was at risk of being attacked by a random crazy person. "You can protect me. Come with me."

He frowned. “I have this shoot set up.” He briefly touched her hand and kissed her forehead. “Go with Hunter. Go on. For me, so I don’t have to worry about you.”

Melanie felt like a five-year-old being sent off to kindergarten against her will. There was no arguing with him. He wouldn’t change his mind, not with a terminal full of nude volunteers. Sometimes she wondered if she were cut out for the role of Artist’s Girlfriend, because the whole slave-to-the-muse thing got old really quickly. But it was flattering that he was worried about her safety. She sighed. “Call me when you board your flight. Have a good shoot.”

“Thanks, Mel. You’re the best.” He turned and left, going over to Sam, his assistant, and leaving Melanie standing there feeling incredibly defeated.

But there was no sense crying over it. She turned and gave Hunter a smile. “Hi, I’m Melanie. Nice to meet you.”

“Hunter.” He shook her hand. No smile.

Which ticked her off a bit. Sure, he was on the job, but the man was going to Mexico to sit on his butt and watch her splay her body out on a beach towel. It was a cake job—she wasn’t really in danger. That was total paranoia on Ian’s part. Even if Savannah knew who she was, she wasn’t likely to hop a plane to Cancún to track her down. That required cash and a passport, and the average stalker wasn’t going to add international travel to their bag of harassing tricks. So why did Hunter look so sour?

“This might be the most boring assignment you’ve ever had,” she warned him as she retrieved the handle of her carry-on and started walking toward their gate.

"Possibly. But I've had a lot of less-than-exciting assignments."

Excuse me? She shot him a sideways glance. He didn't look as if he was making a joke, which led her to the conclusion that he might simply be a jerk. A good-looking jerk, mind you, but a jerk nonetheless. What, as if it was her fault she wasn't a celebrity or a political figure surrounded by pushy paparazzi and people with agendas? She was just a PR rep from Kentucky. Who didn't need a bodyguard, plain and simple. Then again, the man was just doing his job, and she could respect that. "Well, I hope you packed your trunks, since we're going to Mexico. It's better than being stuck here, that's for sure."

"I have to agree with you."

She had a thought. "Do you have a gun on you? Is that legal?"

"I have a license to carry concealed, but no, I did not bring a gun."

"Good." That was reassuring. She didn't want to be detained and body probed by TSA at any point on this trip. That was not the kind of probing she'd had in mind at all. "You do know this is all totally ridiculous, right? My boyfriend is being overly protective." Ian had never been like that in the past, but it was warming her girl bits now, she had to admit.

Hunter gave her a look she couldn't decipher. Lord, the man was attractive. If she were single, she'd want a piece of that. He was the very definition of tall, dark and handsome. Smoking hot. Like five-alarm, sweet and spicy Texas barbecue hot. Finger-licking good.

He must hit the gym every day, because the man had muscles that were no accident. He'd gotten those biceps by sweating, hard. Melanie began to perspire just picturing it, which was startling and completely inappropriate. She wasn't normally one who went for bulked-up manly men, but Hunter's physique paired with that suit was quite a winning combination. His jaw was strong, his eyes an intriguing shade of green. Not that fake contact-lens green you sometimes saw, but a true mossy shade, with flecks of gold.

Yes, the man had been whacked with a sexy stick, and she could appreciate looking without wanting to touch.

Too bad he had zero personality.

And why did she care anyway? She had a boyfriend. A distracted, moody boyfriend, who had stuck her with this hunk of hotness for the next twelve-plus hours. It was nice to know Ian trusted her, she supposed. She wasn't sure she would have if their positions were reversed. But then again, he had no reason to be insecure. Melanie frequently worried that maybe she was more into Ian than he was into her. That was a thought she quickly banished, though.

"If you say so," Hunter told her.

What was that supposed to mean?

He glanced down at his phone, then gestured to their right. "This is our gate. Perfect timing. We're boarding."

"Okay." She started to veer off in the direction of the restroom for a preflight potty break, but squawked when Hunter grabbed her arm and pulled her to a stop.

"Where are you going?" he asked.

Melanie blinked up at him, giving a pointed glance down at his hand, still holding her arm. "To use the toilet," she said bluntly, hoping that would make him back off.

It didn't.

"You can go on the plane," he told her.

"You think someone would buy a plane ticket to get past security just so they could assault me in the ladies' room?"

"I wouldn't rule it out."

"Then you live in a sad little world," she told him. But she obediently got into the boarding line with him. Once Ian arrived in Cancún, there would be none of this nonsense. They were going to hole up in their hotel suite and bang like bunnies, Hunter nowhere in sight.

She hoped anyway. Things hadn't been stellar in the bunny-banging department lately. Or any department, for that matter. It was worrisome. She wasn't ready to pack it in on her relationship with Ian, even if he was often distracted. Even if it had to be a secret. That would be like admitting defeat, and she didn't do defeat, even when she felt defeated.

Fifteen minutes later she was settled in her seat next to her stony-faced bodyguard. A bodyguard. It made her feel pretentious and ridiculous. Not to mention somewhat like a prisoner. While she struggled to stuff her very large purse under the seat in front of her, Hunter sat and watched. She could feel his eyes on her as she heaved and hoed, her blond hair falling in her eyes. When she finally sat back up, he just silently handed her an envelope.

"What is this?" she asked, confused yet again.

"I don't know. I was told to give it to you once the cabin door closed."

A wisp of fear slithered up her spine. That sounded

sketchy, but she instantly dismissed the thought. The envelope was the kind that greeting cards came in. Maybe it was a romantic note from Ian, a gesture to make up for his complete failure to understand how important this vacation was to her.

Turning her back slightly on Hunter so he couldn't read over her shoulder, she opened the envelope and pulled out a card. Not a pretty vellum paper card, but the cards they used at the office to send personal notes. It was one of Ian's mass nudes depicting a dozen people in a tree. Decidedly less promising. She recognized Ian's handwriting inside.

Dear Melanie,
I think we both know this isn't working. To delay the inevitable in Cancún doesn't make any sense. We've had a good run but it's time to move on, and consciously uncouple. Enjoy the beach, and I'll see you at work when you get back.
Best,
Ian

Melanie read it three times, her heart racing as she tried to convince herself there was another meaning to it. But there wasn't. Ian was breaking up with her. On work stationery. After putting her on a plane with a bodyguard.

"Oh, my God," she said before she could stop herself. She grappled for her seat belt, unbuckling it. "I have to go." She couldn't sit here; she couldn't go to Mexico. She needed to get off this plane, away from all these people. She needed to breathe deeply somewhere in private, getting control of her emotions. After she tracked down Ian in Concourse B and asked him how he could be so damn insensitive as to dump her in a Dear Melanie letter.

Then punched him in the no-nos.

This couldn't be happening.

"What are you doing?" Hunter asked her. "We're about to take off. Put your seat belt back on."

"I have to get off this plane," she insisted.

"Are you sick? Afraid of flying?"

She shook her head, panicking, unable to speak. Ian had purposely waited until she was trapped on board so she couldn't even discuss it with him. It was mind-blowing and insulting and vomit inducing.

Hunter's hand settled on the back of her neck, big and warm, gently urging her head forward toward the seat-back tray. "Breathe," he commanded. "Take a deep breath, nice and slow. You're okay."

He had a deep voice, smooth. It commanded obedience, so she did as he said, sucking in a lungful of air and letting it back out through her nose.

"Again," he said.

After a few breaths, she felt marginally better. And like a complete idiot. "I'm sorry."

The plane was backing up off the tarmac and heading for the runway. She was going to Mexico whether she wanted to or not.

"Don't apologize. A lot of people are afraid of flying." His hand massaged the back of her neck. "Are you okay?"

She nodded and sat up again, hoping he'd take his hand off her. While it felt good to have him kneading the knots out of her neck, she was acutely aware of how unfitting it was. He got the hint and dropped his hand. Bracing herself, she turned to look at him, still clutching the stupid note from Ian in her sweaty palm. Those green eyes were gazing at her calmly, and with concern. Maybe Hunter wasn't such a jerk after all.

"What did Ian tell you?" she asked. She needed to know if Hunter had been aware of Ian's plan, so she would know if she needed to die of humiliation or not. "About this trip?"

"That he has a stalker and you're in danger. I got the file on her so I know what she looks like. You don't need to worry."

"I'm not worried about Savannah." She wasn't. Savannah would be where Ian was, not where Melanie was. "I think you coming with me is pointless. No offense."

The corner of his mouth turned up. "None taken. But I've been hired to do a job, whether you think it's necessary or not."

"Ian's not coming," she told him flatly. There was no way to cover it up. If he didn't know now, he'd figure it out by nightfall.

But there was no reaction. Just a blank stare. "Was he supposed to come with you? I was under the impression you were taking the trip solo for R & R."

Excellent. Wonderful. This was officially the vacation from hell. And the ironic thing? She had paid for it. She had put the whole goddamn tab on her credit card as a grand gesture to let Ian know she valued him and their relationship. Even though he was a millionaire and she made thirty grand a year, she had taken on the bill. For love.

Now she was going on vacation with a total stranger who was witness to Ian consciously uncoupling them.

Which was about the douchiest way to say "dumping you" ever recorded in the history of relationships. Had cavemen done this? Sent a wooly mammoth with a stone slab and a broken heart on it to their significant others? She wouldn't be surprised.

A tear escaped, rolling down her cheek. She took a deep, shuddering breath. "He broke up with me. In a note."

She wouldn't have chosen Hunter as a confidant, but she was torn between embarrassment and the need to vent. Since there was no girlfriend convenient and she couldn't use her cell phone on the flight, he was her only option. The disgust and hurt couldn't be contained. "Can you believe that? After a year. A stupid note. One small paragraph." Shaking the note, she added, "And he wrote it on the inside of naked people. It just adds insult to injury."

Then without meaning to, she began to flat-out sob.

HUNTER RYAN WATCHED with horror as Melanie's face screwed up and she started sobbing silently, lip trembling and chest heaving. Oh, God. He really hated when women cried. But hell, he couldn't blame her. What kind of an asshole dumped his girlfriend in a note? He wasn't sure what she meant about the naked people, but given what the guy did for a living, he assumed it had something to do with his work.

A quick note. Jeez.

Not only was it beyond cruel to do that to Melanie, it was rude to do to him, too. Hunter was a bodyguard, not a counselor. He'd been in the marines, where the official motto was Always Faithful, and the unofficial ones were Ignore Your Feelings, followed closely by

Don't Talk About It. And yet somehow he found himself in these situations again and again. He was resisting the urge to unclick his own seat belt and bolt. Unfortunately, there was nowhere to go. They were speeding down the runway at that very moment, and as they took off into the air, he put his hand on Melanie's knee and patted her because he didn't know what else to do.

He valiantly tried to defuse the situation.

"I guess he wanted to avoid confrontation." Hunter figured just about every guy had been there a time or two, not wanting a crying woman on their hands. Or worse, a raging one. He certainly had, but that was when he was sixteen, though. Not thirty. Even he, who—by his ex-girlfriend Danielle's account—was emotionally stunted, was always straightforward with women.

"Avoid confrontation? Do I look confrontational?" she asked, her voice rising higher with each word. "I kept our relationship a secret for a year! I let him travel all over the country without me. I didn't say anything about the fact that his entire job revolves around seeing women naked!"

She had a point or three, and he'd made it worse. There really was no justification for what Bainbridge had done, because clearly he had planned it at least a week in advance, which was when he'd hired Hunter.

Okay, retreat carefully. Make it clear he was on her side. He knew how to do this. He'd spent his entire childhood negotiating the land mines of his mother's lousy relationships. "You don't look confrontational. At all. Personally, I think it's disrespectful to break up with someone in a note. Only a real dick would do that."

But she balked. "I wouldn't say he's a *dick*. That seems harsh."

Proving yet again that no matter what he said, it was always the wrong thing. Why did women contradict everything, even when the guys were agreeing with them? Then wonder why men didn't want to communicate? He looked at her, unsure how to proceed. "He told me he wasn't coming, but I thought you knew. I did not know he was going to do this or I wouldn't have agreed to be the messenger. As far as I'm concerned, what he did to you and what he did to me, essentially making me a party to his dirty work, makes him a dick."

Her lip trembled. Shit. But then she nodded. "You're right. He is a dick. I was dating a dick and didn't even know it. I'm such an idiot."

Hunter's face hurt. He was the last person in the world to be giving anyone advice on relationships. Before Danielle he had dated Lynn for four years, but for three and a half of those he'd been deployed to another hemisphere. He had no business doling out advice, but really all Melanie needed was some reassurance she was not in the wrong, which she wasn't.

"You're not an idiot. You couldn't have known he was going to do this. It's his issue that he's too wimpy to speak to you face-to-face, not yours."

And that was all he was going to say about it. He was done with this conversation—stick a fork in him. It made him uncomfortable and reminded him of many nights as a kid watching his mother cry and eat ice cream straight from the container after yet another failed attempt at happily-ever-after. There was no happily-ever-after, end of story. So while he didn't want to be a dick himself, he wanted Melanie to phone a friend when they got to Mexico and leave him out of it.

He had sworn off relationships himself since Danielle. Before her had been Lynn, and before Lynn there was Allison. All three had left him, and he figured after three strikes, he was out. It wasn't his game. He was determined that short-term hookups would be his new reality, and if Melanie wanted honest advice, that was what he would tell her. But she wouldn't. No one wanted to hear his cynical thoughts on love.

She nodded, still sniffling. When she bent over to root around in her bag again, her shirt rode up, exposing the small of her back and the curve of her backside. Hunter cleared his throat, shifting uncomfortably. The one thing he definitely had not bargained on was finding his client attractive. Melanie was beautiful, even when she was crying. She had delicate features and plump pink lips that lured his thoughts straight into dangerous territory. Her tight jeans and loose-fitting shirt called attention to the fact that she was petite and feminine and curvy in all the right ways.

When he'd taken the assignment, he'd been led to believe Melanie was going alone by choice, and he'd anticipated being treated like an employee. That was fine with him, because it was a job, and he needed the work. But this scenario was far worse, hands down. There was no buffer. No way to remain remote and silent in the background, which was what he preferred. He was stuck making awkward conversation and poor attempts at comforting her broken heart. This was worse than Afghanistan. Okay, not really, but it was worse than the time he'd gotten heat rash on his jock. He was squirming just as badly.

Melanie sat back up, having retrieved a tissue, which she was using to dab at her eyes. Makeup was streaked on her cheeks. Hunter decided that if it had been him, he would have waited until after the vacation to break things off. What the hell was wrong with Ian Bainbridge that he didn't want to spend a week with Melanie in a bikini? That prospect was the only redeeming thing about this work assignment. She was sweet, though, too, so what was Ian's problem? Why would he let this woman get onto a plane without him?

The guy clearly had issues.

Hunter had issues, too, but according to his exes, his were more along the lines of inability to communicate his feelings and failure to be romantic. He wasn't a commitmentphobe. Nor was he a dick. He would be perfectly happy to spend a week on a beach with a sexy girlfriend, if he had one. Which he did not.

"I mean, am I that stupid?" Melanie asked him, still dabbing at her eyes. "The truth is, I knew things weren't great between us. The whole point of this stupid vacation was to fix the problems in our relationship. That really worked. Not. And now I'm out a ton of money."

"At least you didn't get pregnant," he said. "That's a really expensive way to save a relationship." He meant it as a joke, but she gave him a look that indicated he was in no way funny. He mentally kneed himself in the nuts. He knew better than to tease a woman who was crying. Years of his mother's dating had taught him that, but maybe he had been in the desert too long.

"Don't joke about being pregnant. That's like tempting fate." But then her face screwed up. "Not that I can possibly be pregnant, given it's been six weeks since we had sex."

Oh, no. This was not information he wanted. Because now he didn't know what to do with it.

"I'm sorry. What I said was in poor taste." He yanked a magazine out of the seat pocket in front of him and handed it to her. "Why don't you read something and try to distract yourself?"

She blinked and eyed the magazine he was holding out to her without taking it. "*Skymiles?* You think vibrating massage chairs and cat condos for sale are going to distract me from the fact that I mean absolutely and utterly nothing to the man I care about?"

"You'll never know unless you try." He was damn hopeful she would.

Shaking her head, she gave a watery laugh. "No, thanks. I'd rather wallow."

Not him. He'd rather be eaten alive by piranhas than sit in his own misery. He'd perfected the art of avoiding grief and disappointment. "Well, you wallow away, then, without me interfering. I'll read the magazine." He opened it up and stared blankly at an extensive gate system that was for…dogs? He wasn't sure. What he was sure of was that he didn't want to talk anymore.

He felt for the girl, he really did. It wasn't that he couldn't sympathize, but he knew how this went. She would lament and rail and sink into self-doubt and he would nod and express sympathy and tell her she was worth so much more—which she was—and he would be exhausted and she wouldn't believe him anyway. He'd done this. He was that guy, the one every woman went to for advice, which they all subsequently ignored.

But the last thing he wanted to talk about right now was relationships, when he was determined to give up on the concept altogether.

Melanie was silent for a whopping sixty seconds before she sighed loudly and said, "Maybe when we get to Mexico I should turn around and go home."

As much as Hunter wanted to end this conversation, he couldn't let *that* go. "Can you get a refund on your trip?"

"No."

"Then why would you go home to the snow and cold? Enjoy the vacation, Melanie, as much as you can. Don't let Ian ruin your time off work."

"I even booked excursions," she said, sounding so forlorn he wanted to put his arm around her and pull her against his chest for a hug. Like the guy who listens and gives advice. Damn his mother. She'd done this to him.

"Who goes zip-lining by themselves? It's pathetic."

"I'll go with you."

"You will?" She blinked up at him with hopeful eyes.

"Of course. It's my job."

That was the wrong thing to say. She made a face. "Great. So I have a paid companion. Even better."

"I'd do it even if I wasn't being paid." But it was too little too late. He shoved the magazine back into the pocket in front of him. This was going to be a long-ass trip with no relief in sight, and the ibuprofen he'd taken for his bum arm wasn't going to be any help.

She gave a snort. "Thanks."

He didn't know what to say then, so he said nothing.

After a minute, she said, "You know what chaps my ass?"

"Uh, no." He couldn't even begin to guess.

"I was forcing myself to love Ian. Can you believe that?" She was shredding the tissue in her lap, a little pile gathering on top of her seat belt buckle. "It all seemed so good on paper, and when I pictured myself with a man, it was always with an artistic type, not a macho man. Yet I never really *loved* Ian, not like I was supposed to."

"Well, that's great," he said, suddenly feeling a whole lot better about the next week. Maybe this meant he wasn't in for seven solid days of tears after all. "So you weren't really meant to be with him. Better to know that now rather than later." Though he wished it hadn't been on his watch.

"I wouldn't say it's great. It's still humiliating and hurtful. I mean, I was willing to try. To nurture our relationship and let it grow. Why wasn't he?"

"You're not a tree," he told her bluntly. "It doesn't grow. It's either there or it isn't."

"What, like love at first sight?"

"No. But chemistry, attraction. Admiration. Driving and compelling interest. That's all there from the jump. If it's not, you can't force it." Hell, he should know. With the exception of his first serious relationship, he'd taken the rational, think with your head, not your heart approach and it hadn't worked. Danielle had been right when she'd said he lacked emotion. They both had been remote because they didn't have that intense interest in each other.

She frowned. "How do you know if it's there or not?"

Was she serious? Hunter felt his eyebrows shoot up. "You know. Don't tell me you don't know when you find someone attractive." Like he found her. God, her lips looked as though they'd been made for kissing. Did she realize that? Apparently not.

"Well, sure. I guess. I mean, I look at you and I can see that you're an attractive man, but that doesn't mean we'd be compatible."

Hunter thought she was missing the point. It was more than that. Way more. But he didn't mind hearing that she found him attractive. "I'm not just talking about physical attraction."

"Are you saying you don't find me physically attractive?" Melanie bundled up all her tissue scraps and tossed them in her purse with more force than was necessary.

Minefields. Everywhere he walked with women. "That is not what I was saying. At all. Yes, I find you physically attractive." Which was an understatement. She actually came pretty close to his image of the ideal woman with her blond hair, her juicy mouth, her perky breasts and narrow waist. She made him want to protect her from harm, and at the same time he wanted to push her up against a wall and make her scream with pleasure. But telling her that would be completely unprofessional. He was still on a job. "You're a beautiful woman."

"I don't feel beautiful. I feel foolish. And a little airsick."

Yikes. That was all they needed. "Here. Lie down and close your eyes." He patted his legs, indicating that she should stretch out.

"You don't mind?"

He minded a lot of things, but despite his desperate desire to stay remote with his client, he didn't want her getting sick. Plus that indescribable "it" he had mentioned to her? He felt it. That tug of chemistry, of desire, in both his groin and his chest. He was attracted to her, yes, but he also felt…interest.

Not good. Not good at all.

Which made offering for her to sprawl across his lap incredibly stupid. When she did, her body felt warm and soft on his hard thighs. She glanced up at him with big brown eyes. "You're very hard."

"Excuse me?" He wasn't there yet, but if she kept shifting around like that, he would be, and she'd get an earful.

"Your legs. They're very muscular. Not the best pillow."

Right.

She smiled up at him. "But thank you. I appreciate it." Squeezing his knee, she added, "You're sweet."

Hunter grunted in response. She closed her eyes.

And his job, among other things down south, got a whole hell of a lot harder than he could have ever predicted.

2

It had been a mistake to lie on Hunter's legs. Melanie kept her eyes closed, but not to sleep. It was to avoid looking at him. She was very aware of how close she was to his crotch, and how firm his body was under hers. His hand resting on her side was enormous, heavy, warm. She felt surrounded by him, protected.

And he smelled like the woods. As if he'd chopped a cord of firewood, thrown on a suit and jumped on a plane, all without skipping a beat. It was appealing.

There was something dangerous about this. She was vulnerable. Hurt. Embarrassed. Hunter was sexy and very masculine. She didn't want to fall into that trap of needing to prove she was feminine and desirable by having rebound sex. Not that Hunter wanted to have sex with her. Despite saying he found her attractive, he'd been looking at her like he was in pain since the minute he'd met her. She was sure he'd simply been tossing out a compliment because he felt sorry for her and she'd backed him into a corner.

So even if she wanted to make the massive mistake of using Hunter to make her feel better about herself, it wasn't going to work. He wasn't interested. Though he was being very nice in a pained, aloof sort of way.

He was patient and he was trying to offer sympathy. Despite her deep humiliation, she needed to pull herself together and not make Hunter pay for Ian's sins. Ian was back at the airport blithely doing what he loved to do and leaving a total stranger to clean up his mess. She hoped Hunter was being adequately paid for his time.

Shifting slightly on his lap, she evened out her breathing and reflected. She was ashamed to realize that she had been trying to salvage a union that had never stood a chance in the first place. Sure, she cared about Ian, but how well did she really know him? There had been compatibility, yet no connection. Why had she been so willing to settle for that, and why did it still hurt so much? She'd never thought of herself as having a fragile ego, but apparently she did.

Maybe it wouldn't have been so painful if Ian had taken her out to dinner and told her face-to-face. They could have discussed it, mutually agreed that something was off, given each other a mature and slightly sad kiss goodbye and gotten on with their lives. This was different. This was bullshit. This was her only vacation for the year and Ian had ruined it summarily, without cause or concern. Hunter was right. Ian was a dick. Sad to think she'd devoted a year to a dick, and not even the good kind.

Which suddenly made her aware of how long it had been since she'd had sex. And how close she was to Hunter's penis. Her thoughts went full circle.

She decided to sit up.

Hunter gave her a look of surprise. "You okay?"

"I have to go to the restroom." It was a lie. She just needed to evacuate his lap before her thoughts took a turn into the gutter. It was as if her body had been all primed for booty on this vacation, and her hormones weren't about to back down now that plans had changed. Even though Hunter couldn't read her mind, she felt self-conscious.

"That's right, you had to go before we boarded." Hunter unclicked his seat belt and stood up in the aisle so she could scoot past him.

"Thanks." She eased out of the seat and started down the aisle. Locking herself in the microscopic restroom, she glanced in the mirror and almost passed out. Good gravy, she looked like hell in a handbasket. Her face was swollen and splotchy and her hair was a disaster from running her hands through it nervously. There was no way Hunter was going to be attracted to her now that she'd taken a ride on the Hot Mess Express.

After splashing water on her face, she tried to pat her hair down, but it was hopeless. She hadn't brought her purse with her, so there was no real way to repair the damage. Not that lip gloss was going to change the fact that her eyes were swollen and her nose was stuffy. She rolled her neck and shoulders and tried to swallow the reality that she was winging her way to Mexico with a man who was a total stranger. There was no turning back, no getting out of it.

She would literally be paying for this vacation for the next six months at least, so she could either lock herself in her hotel room and cry, or she could reset her idea of what the trip was going to be and try to enjoy it. She was still leaving winter behind. She didn't have to work. There would be dessert buffets and salsa dancing. And while Hunter wasn't going to be kissing her naked body, he was far better company than, say, her mother. Or a crying baby. Or a baboon. All of those would be worse options for travel companions.

A sexy stranger should not be a hardship.

Opening the restroom door with the violent shove it required, she went back down the aisle carefully, determined to make the best of things and to try to get to know Hunter a little better. The poor man was saddled with an awkward work assignment, aka *her*, so the least she could do was try to make the whole thing less awful for both of them.

He began to stand as she approached so she could reach her window seat, but she waved him back down. "I can squeeze past. Don't worry about it." She felt guilty enough about falling apart on him.

But right as she started to maneuver her way by, they hit a pocket of turbulence and the plane jumped. Knocked off balance, Melanie gave a small cry of alarm and tried to grab the seat in front of her. Too late. She fell against Hunter with all the grace of a hippo doing ballet. She didn't land in his lap. That would have been better. No, instead she basically shoved her butt right on up against his chest.

Scrambling and stumbling, she pulled her body away from him and tried to throw herself at her seat. Hunter put his hands on her hips.

"Steady," he said.

Right. Steady. That was her. Hair in her eyes, she shifted to the right. But he had shifted as well, and somehow she managed to knock her hip into his arm. "Sorry," she said, breathless. She turned to face him and blew her hair off her face. "These seats are really narrow."

He looked more amused than irritated. "I could have just stood up."

"I didn't want to inconvenience you," she said, bracing herself as the plane lurched again. She stood between his legs, his hands still on her waist. "Shall we dance?" she joked.

"The only kind of dance I know that starts out like this is a lap dance," he said wryly.

Oh, jeez. Her cheeks burned. She did not want him to think she was flirting. "I was thinking more along the lines of the rumba. Clearly we spend our weekends in different ways."

Hunter laughed.

It was the first time he had, and it was a deep, rumbling, pleasant sound.

Melanie smiled at him. For the first time since Ian had told her he wasn't getting on that flight with her, she didn't feel as though she was on the verge of losing it.

"Lap rumba?" he asked. "It's all about compromise."

"Because I'm so graceful." She made another move toward her seat and, as if to prove her point, managed to bump his arm on the way by.

He winced.

"Oh! Sorry." Now she was causing him pain. "Are you okay? Did my butt pop your arm out of the socket or something? I've always been something of a klutz."

Back in her seat at last, she turned to see him shaking his head.

"It's just an old injury. Don't worry about it."

"Really? How did you hurt yourself?"

"I fell out of a Humvee after we hit a mine and broke my arm in four places."

She wasn't exactly well versed in vehicles but she was pretty sure that was what they drove in the military. "Wow, that sounds painful. So you were in the service? How long have you been out?"

"Three months."

That was way more recent than she would have expected. "Oh! So you had a long career, then. What made you decide to leave—your injury?"

He gave her a look she couldn't decipher. "Are you calling me old?"

She rolled her eyes. "No. But you're clearly not twenty-two, either. I just meant it wasn't as if you did a few years and got out. It was a commitment."

"It was. Twelve years. I would still be serving if it wasn't for my injury. I realized it was time to pack it in. I just turned thirty."

There was the rub. Not her comment, but his own fear of aging. Of starting a new life and career and feeling superfluous. "Thirty is the new twenty."

"Now you're calling me immature."

But the corner of his mouth turned up.

"I'm trying to get to know you," she said, nudging his knee with hers. "Stop being difficult about it."

"Why the hell would you want to get to know me? I'm your bodyguard."

"You're my only company for the next seven days." The look he gave her was so pained she laughed. "Thanks for being so thrilled." Then a thought occurred to her. "Wait, you are staying the whole time, aren't you?"

The thought of him leaving after just a couple of days upset her, and she wasn't entirely sure why.

"Yes, I'm staying. But I thought you said you weren't afraid of Ian's stalker."

"I'm not. I'm afraid of being…bored." Alone. She was afraid to be alone.

That was an unnerving thought to have. Was that why she'd been willing to settle for the half-assed attention of Ian Bainbridge? Because having a boyfriend, even one who was never around, was better than not having one at all? God, she wasn't in middle school anymore.

She wasn't that needy. She knew she wasn't. But she was a woman who thought that she could organize everything in her life, including romance. She lived by lists, and Ian had ticked all the boxes on her checklist of what her ideal partner should be.

"How can you be bored when you have zip-lining to try?"

There was that. She wasn't even going to mention that she'd also signed up for exploring Mayan ruins and horseback riding on the beach. Her credit card must be on fire.

"You shouldn't go zip-lining with me with your injury, by the way. I can go by myself." She didn't want to guilt her bodyguard into doing something that would set his recovery back.

"I can go freaking zip-lining. I'm not paralyzed. Hell, even paralyzed I could still do it."

Uh-oh. She'd pierced his male pride. "Don't get your panties in a wad. I was trying to let you off the hook, not imply you're incapable." She couldn't help but add, "And you could reinjure yourself."

"I'm fine." He undid his seat belt and leaned forward.

"Where are you going?" Melanie asked, suddenly

panicking. Was he leaving? Not that he had anywhere *to* go. But she wasn't sure she wanted to be alone with her thoughts now any more than she wanted to be alone on tourist excursions.

"I'm taking my jacket off. It's hotter than hell in here."

He sounded irritable.

"Oh. Here." She reached up and turned his airflow on.

"Thanks." Hunter did his best to shake off his jacket in the tight space.

It was tempting to help him as he struggled out of it, but she figured his balls might shrivel up and fall off if she did. Why did men feel so emasculated by accepting help? And good God, how tempting was it to touch those arms? He was wearing a light blue dress shirt, so she didn't have the greatest view of his biceps, but without the jacket it was clear that despite what he'd said, he'd brought the guns. Jeez Louise.

"So…you didn't bring any swimwear?" she asked, striving for casual. Any heterosexual woman past puberty and under the age of, oh, death would want to take a gander at him without a shirt. It was just reality, and she wasn't about to feel guilty about it. Much. It might fall under the category of objectifying him, but at least she wasn't paying his salary. No boss-employee conflict of interest here.

Not that she was doing anything other than looking. She was getting to know him. As a potential friend. That was it. She had to remember that and not throw herself at his hard, gorgeous body.

Damn it. Where was the flight attendant with the service cart? She needed some water.

HUNTER REALLY NEEDED a glass of water. Between the small confines of the plane and the fact that Melanie didn't seem to understand how attractive she was or what she was doing to him every time she brushed against him, he was burning up. When her ass, perfectly cupped in those tight jeans, had bumped against his chest, it had taken all of his willpower to keep from pulling her down onto his lap for a more enjoyable plane ride for both of them.

He shifted his jacket over his erection and put his seat-back tray down, as well. Anything to hide his embarrassing state of arousal. This was a job. She was a client. It wasn't her fault that he hadn't gotten laid in fourteen months. Fourteen long, celibate, lonely months. He'd been pumped to get home from Afghanistan despite the arm, because he didn't need two functioning arms to take his girlfriend to bed. All those months he'd been fantasizing and waiting for the moment when he could nail Danielle again, and he'd gotten home with his cast off and his libido primed. But instead of a weekend sex fest, he'd gotten dumped.

"I brought a pair of trunks, sure. I have to blend in and look as though I belong on the beach." He was going to be sitting in a beach chair watching Melanie in her bathing suit. He was praying for a bikini. It just had to be a bikini.

"Good point." She smiled at him. "Is applying sunscreen part of your official duties? I can never reach that spot right here." Twisting, she tried to reach between her shoulder blades. "Here." She twisted again, her chest pushing out toward him, breasts taunting him. Laughing, she added, "See? It's a problem. I don't want to burn."

It was then and there that Hunter decided that this was bullshit. Ian Bainbridge had only hired him for one week, and hadn't even paid him yet. He didn't owe the guy total professionalism, not when Ian hadn't been completely up front with him about the situation. Fourteen months was too long to go without sex, and Melanie was probably equally disappointed at the prospect of a celibate vacation. There was no way he could be expected to spend a whole week alone with her and not die of sexual frustration.

That left him two choices: he could settle her into the resort then turn around and go home, or he could convince her that what they both needed was a no-strings-attached week of sex and sunshine.

The first choice seemed unethical, since Ian believed there was a possibility Melanie was in danger. Hunter wouldn't be able to live with himself if something happened to her, no matter how remote the possibility. The second option was maybe just a little sketchy and inappropriate, but they were both adults and he wasn't going to twist her arm too hard. Just…coax.

What would Melanie be like in bed? He had a feeling she would approach sex without guile, but with a certain amount of efficiency. She would want the right location and the right time, and she would have a checklist. Foreplay, oral sex, penetration, orgasm, done. Maybe he was wrong—he'd only known her an hour—but it was a gut feeling, a hunch. He had a sudden visual of her approaching his cock with a look of purpose.

It made him hard, and it made him want to show her that sex didn't need an order or a plan. "I can be your cabana boy," he told her. "I'll rub anywhere you want."

Her eyebrows shot up in surprise. "Thanks. Um. So…tell me about yourself. Are you married? Children?"

He almost grinned, but held it back. "No and no." Pride had him instinctively withholding the information about Danielle, but then he realized it could work to his advantage. "When I got home from my deployment, my girlfriend ended things."

There it was. Her face softened and her hand came to rest on his knee. "Oh, I'm sorry. It must have been hard to make a long-distance relationship work."

"Lots of people manage to," he said truthfully. "So I guess it just wasn't meant to be." Though she could have told him that before he spent months anticipating a happy homecoming.

"You are very stoic, then."

She didn't ask it as a question. "No. I wouldn't say that. I just go to the rifle range and shoot things to work it out."

"That sounds healthy." She made a face at him. "Maybe you need a creative outlet instead."

"Maybe I need sex." See what she did with that.

"Oh!" Her cheeks turned pink. "Well. True. There's that."

"Can I get you anything to drink?" the cheerful flight attendant asked, locking her cart into place next to Hunter.

It was perfect timing. Let Melanie ponder what he'd said for a while.

"I'll take a coffee. Black. And a water." He turned to Melanie. "What would you like?"

"Just a club soda," she said. "With a lime. And vodka."

Oh, really? "Somebody's ready to party," he said, amused.

"It is kind of early, isn't it?" she said. "But hell, I'm from Kentucky. I know how to hold my liquor. I stand by my choice."

"That's eight dollars," the flight attendant said discreetly. "Only credit cards." She bent over and pulled out a tiny liquor bottle.

Hunter got out his wallet and handed her a credit card while Melanie was still wrestling her jumbo purse out from under the seat.

"You don't have to do that," she protested.

"Honey, if the man wants to buy you a drink, let him," the flight attendant said, handing over both glasses. "You'll never see him again, so there's no expectation."

"We're going to Mexico together for a week," Melanie told her.

The flight attendant made a sound and waved her hand. "Well, in that case, he should be buying all your drinks. I'm sorry, I didn't realize you were a couple." She turned to Hunter. "I thought you were a business traveler."

"I'm her bodyguard," he said, because he felt as if he needed to explain his suit. Plus it would drive Melanie crazy.

"Are you serious?" The woman eyed Melanie more carefully. "Are you famous?"

When Melanie started to shake her head no, Hunter touched her knee. "She's not famous to the average person. But those who know who she is are such rabid fans she's accumulated some stalkers. I'm here to protect her."

"Oh. My." The flight attendant unlocked her cart and started to push it. She asked Melanie in a low voice, "Can I ask what industry you're in?"

Hunter didn't expect Melanie to play along. He thought she would bluster and apologize and say it was really her boyfriend the famous photographer who had a stalker. But she stunned him by nodding solemnly and saying, "Sure. I'm an adult-film star. Maybe you've seen some of my work? *Poke Her Haunches?* Or maybe *Romeo, Juliet and Juliet*?"

The curious smile disappeared. "No, I haven't." The cart moved rapidly three feet down the aisle.

Coughing to cover his laugh, Hunter looked at Melanie in amusement. "I wasn't aware of your history."

"I don't like to brag," she said breezily.

"Home videos? Or can I download them online?" He knew she was joking, but without warning an image of Melanie in a corset and touching his sword ambushed his thoughts.

She smacked his leg. "Neither. You goof."

"I'm a goof, am I? You're the one messing with the flight attendant." He eyed her carefully. "Be honest, you wouldn't even make a home video. That's not your style."

"Hey! What do you know about my style?"

"You don't seem like an impulsive person. Making a sex tape at home is usually for couples who are spontaneous. Or daring."

"I could be daring."

His assessment seemed to have annoyed her. Or at least made her slightly defensive.

"I mean, I have posed naked, you know," she said.

"Your boyfriend is a photographer. I don't find that particularly daring."

"My *ex*-boyfriend is a photographer. Past-tense boyfriend. Not my boyfriend anymore."

Hunter felt like a jerk. "I'm sorry. I didn't mean to bring up a sore subject."

She shrugged. "I didn't just pose for him at his place alone. I took part in all his shoots. It was like our private joke. I had to travel with him anyway for work, so there I am, in every photo he's done for the past year."

"Really? You're like Where's Waldo? Only naked?" That was a tantalizing thought. Holy hell. The chick had guts. And was clearly comfortable in her own skin, which was incredibly hot.

Melanie laughed, and took a sip of her drink. "Sometimes I wore a disguise."

"How do you wear a disguise when you're naked?" His mind ran in directions that were so dirty he was glad his jacket was still lying in his lap.

"Glasses. A wig."

"Right." Because she wasn't a total pervert like he was. "Fascinating. Here's to you getting naked." He raised his plastic coffee cup and offered her a toast. "For posterity and for art."

"For art." She lifted her own tumbler and clicked it gently against his, giving him a soft, sexy smile.

The minute the plane landed he was going to search the shit out of Ian Bainbridge's photographs online. Wig or no wig, he was certain he would recognize Melanie's sexy curves anywhere.

Thank God for the internet and both Ian's genius as

an artist and his stupidity as a man. This assignment was turning out to be a whole lot more exciting than Hunter had anticipated.

3

Here's to you getting naked. Melanie wished. She wondered if Hunter had any idea how his words were affecting her. He probably didn't mean to be flirtatious but it felt as though the man had been talking about sex nonstop since the minute they'd boarded this godforsaken flight an hour earlier. Or maybe she was just projecting her lack of sex onto the conversation. Either way, it was driving her crazy.

By the way, just who was his moron of an ex-girlfriend? Though she supposed it had been decent of her to wait until he got home to dump him face-to-face, unlike certain photographers who thought a note would suffice. It would have been really cold to end things via text or email while Hunter was on active duty halfway around the world. So maybe the ex wasn't a bitch. Maybe she just wanted something different. Something that wasn't gorgeous.

Melanie couldn't believe she'd told Hunter about being in Ian's photos. She'd never told anyone but her best friend, Jeannie, about that. She had felt bold and sassy doing it, and she'd never felt a need to talk about it. But she had practically bragged to Hunter. Because no matter what logic was telling her, she was attracted to him and she wanted to impress him.

Not wanting to further engage in a conversation that was bound to make her hot and bothered with no way to cool her heat, Melanie dug out the fashion magazine she'd brought with her. Hunter let her flip through the pages in peace, something Ian wouldn't have done. He would have read over her shoulder, criticizing the unnatural state of the models. Not that she didn't agree with him, but sometimes she just wanted to look at the shoes and daydream, not listen to why the lighting in the shot was wrong.

Hmm. Interesting that she was finding herself momentarily relieved that Ian wasn't with her. He was no longer her boyfriend and already she felt past the stage of crying over it. The sheer speed with which she was reaching the stage of acceptance spoke volumes. It also disturbed her. Good grief, she had been willing to convince herself of a whole hell of a lot, hadn't she?

Hunter had his eyes closed, so Melanie studied him surreptitiously. He didn't have a boyish face, but rather one that was chiseled and mature, with pronounced cheekbones and a strong jaw. He had a scar on his chin, just a thin white slash where there was no beard shadow. Most of her adult life had been spent dating men she had deemed creative and artistic. It had been a decade or more since she had allowed herself to look at a man—a real one, not a movie star—and feel primal in her attraction to him. To think that there was something really hot about him purely because of his hard-bodied masculinity and manly scent.

Until now. She felt it acutely as she watched Hunter

sleep. Even unconscious, he radiated strength and virility. On some intrinsic level, her body responded to that.

After watching her friends fall one by one for the bad boys in school, she had been determined to pursue guys who had something to offer intellectually instead of the ones who made her panties heat up. A girl couldn't think with damp drawers, and Melanie wanted to be in control, always. She'd spent the past dozen years keeping her wits about her, but it seemed at some point her wits had gone witless. She'd convinced herself to spend a year dating a man who clearly wasn't worthy of her attention.

She tore up the note from Ian methodically, ripping it in slow, careful strips. She made a pile on her tray, then jammed it into her empty plastic cup. When the flight attendant came back around to prepare them for landing, she handed her the trash, with the note—an uneventful ending to the last year of her love life. As though it had never been.

When they hit the runway, Hunter jerked awake and gave her a sexy, slumberous smile that warmed her from the inside out.

"Bienvenido a México," he said. "I hope you enjoy your vacation, Melanie."

Thoughtful on top of sexy.

"Or should I call you by your adult-film-star name?"

She laughed. "And what would that be?"

"You tell me. Though you look like a Candy to me."

"Why is that?"

"Sweet."

Melanie wasn't sure if she was sweet or not. She liked to think she was nice, but adjectives used to describe her normally ran more along the lines of efficient, organized, punctual. Nothing exciting at all. There wasn't a porn name out there that really suited her. "I'm not feeling it."

"Melly, then. Melly Ambrosia."

"Melly?" It did sound suitably made-up, which was almost a prerequisite for a porn-star name. "I can live with that. So is that our story at the resort? I'm a porn star? No one will buy it when they see me in a bikini."

"Tell people whatever you want. You're on vacation."

"So you keep reminding me." Melanie looked out the window. No snow. The sun was shining. No work to be done. Check. She was on vacation. There was a fruity drink in her future.

She had to admit, as they walked down the stairs of the plane and crossed the runway to the airport entrance, the warm tropical breeze felt amazing on her winter-weary skin. She rolled her shoulders to work out the kinks and raised her face to the sun.

"Ah, that feels so good," she told Hunter. He was carrying his suit jacket over his shoulder and squinting as he walked behind her. "Do you want to go to the pool when we get to the hotel?"

"Whatever you want," he said. "I am here to follow you."

Right. This bullshit bodyguard business. Maybe they needed to discuss that a little further. "How long did Ian hire you for?" If Hunter thought he was going to shadow her back in Chicago, this was going to get old quick. She wanted him to roll around naked in bed with her, not silently follow her as she walked to the coffee shop. That was just weird. And wait—*did* she want Hunter to roll around naked in bed with her?

She glanced back at him. He was rolling up his shirt-sleeves. Yes. Why, yes, she did. Bad Melanie. Or maybe in this case, Melly. If she were pretending to be Melly Ambrosia, adult-film star, would Hunter want to have sex with her? Or would he still see her as nothing more than a boring work assignment?

And if she were assuming a fictional identity in the name of fun and spontaneity, that wasn't like having a pathetic rebound affair, was it? It was her breaking out of her shell, celebrating her newly single status and her ability to have sex whenever she felt like.

That was what it would be. If she did it. Which she wouldn't. But she was certain of one thing—there was no relationship in her immediate future. If she wanted a little boom-boom, it was going to have to be on the condition that they were not dating. Which was in direct contradiction to everything she had done for the past twelve years. When push came to shove, she doubted she could actually go through with the casual-sex thing, which meant her unfortunate and unintentional state of celibacy was going to continue.

It was ridiculous that in a relationship she'd had to suffer unsatisfied. Sex with Ian hadn't been bad, but he had always been a little selfish. It seemed she was a little slow on the uptake if she was just now figuring out there had been about nine million red flags as to why things with Ian hadn't been working. It had looked good on paper, but you couldn't make someone fall for you like a ton of bricks if he didn't want to.

Assessing someone based on data and compatibility was a waste of time. So was being reasonable and waiting for someone else to determine her future. She needed to have a think on this trip and figure out her next move.

"Ian hired me for the week."

Lame. "So my safety only matters for a week while I'm a thousand miles away from home and Ian's stalker? That's just dumb." She shook her head, but then smiled when she was handed a flower by a line of women greeting them.

"I have no answers," Hunter said, accepting a flower from the greeters but then turning to tuck it into Melanie's hair. She shivered at the unexpected touch of his fingertips brushing against her cheek. "I learned a long time ago that we can never get inside someone else's head. It's a waste of time and energy trying."

She gazed up at him, wishing he would touch her again. That simple contact felt so good. "So you aren't wondering what I'm thinking right now?" She wanted him to guess. She wanted him to know that she was attracted to him. Make the first move. She was tired of being the pursuer, of always having to make plans and seek out opportunities to be with a guy. She wanted to be chased. Melly the porn star would be pursued.

He gave her a crooked smile. "If you're Melly Ambrosia, you're thinking you'd like a break from sex. You just want to be left alone to sunbathe and zip-line."

Then clearly she was not Melly Ambrosia, because all she'd been thinking about for weeks was sex and how she wasn't having any. "I would assume porn stars actually like sex."

"I wouldn't know, truthfully. Never having been one myself." His hand had dropped, and he gestured as he started walking. "Baggage claim is this way."

She didn't care about baggage claim, but she fell in step beside him. "Don't be modest."

Hunter laughed. "The military career is not a cover for an illustrious film history. I really was on active duty for twelve years." He glanced over at her and winked. "Though I *could* have been a porn star if I wanted to. I have all the qualifications."

There he was again. Talking about sex in a roundabout way that could be misconstrued if he wasn't careful. "What, the name?"

"That, and the assets." He grinned wickedly.

Classic dude bragging. She wasn't sure if he was flirting, or just being a guy. "The modesty, too." She gestured to where everyone was milling around. "Is this our carousel number?"

"Looks that way. What does your bag look like?"

"It's got polka dots." She already saw it. "There it is." She pointed, then dropped her carry-on bag so she could go for the larger suitcase and haul it off the belt.

But Hunter beat her to it. He yanked her bag off the belt with one hand. She rushed after him. "Hunter! Your arm. I can get it."

"I have two arms," he told her, dropping his jacket onto her now-upright suitcase. "And the bad one works."

She fought the urge to roll her eyes. She wasn't used to manly men and their need to prove they were 100 percent badass at all times. This was going to be an interesting experience. "Thanks for getting it."

He pulled a significantly smaller black bag off the belt.

"That's your suitcase?" she asked. "What's in there, two pairs of underwear and a toothbrush?" She couldn't exist for six hours on a bag that size. Seven days? Forget it.

"Who needs underwear?" he said.

There it was again. Teasing. Flirtation. "As long as you have fresh breath, I guess the rest is none of my business."

Hunter couldn't read Melanie's expression as he led her out to where a shuttle was waiting to take them to the resort. She looked pensive. He had thought he'd pushed it too far teasing her about her porn-star name, so he had retreated behind humor. He needed to remember that she was hurt and feeling bad, sad, mad, whatever, about being sent on this trip solo. She had expected to be there with her boyfriend and instead she'd gotten him. He needed to dial it back a notch, be more sensitive.

Now she was brooding and he wasn't sure why. Was it the whole situation, or was it his stupid underwear joke? She had paused outside to lift her face to the sun and breathed in deeply. Maybe she was just relaxing. Reflecting. He stayed silent throughout the drive and tipped the driver when they arrived at the resort. Rolling both bags behind him, he let her wander into the lobby first, a little surprised at how average the resort was. It wasn't luxurious by any means. So it seemed that on top of Ian's poor timing, he was a boyfriend with a budget. It was a nice resort, and more than adequate for Hunter, but it honestly looked like something he and his small bank account would have chosen, not what a multimillionaire would choose. But hell, maybe Ian didn't like wasting money. Nothing wrong with that.

Frankly, he was glad. He personally felt uncomfortable in a chi-chi environment. Like a bull in a china shop. He didn't have the clothes or the manners or the money to hang with a highbrow crowd, so he was pleased with the way this trip was turning out. What had started out as an onerous task to earn a few bucks was now playing out to be a relaxed and easy week in the sun. With a gorgeous woman.

Who was now raising her voice, upset at the desk clerk.

He set their luggage aside and came up behind her. "What's the matter?" He put a hand on the small of her back, hoping to reassure her. Melanie was tense, a frown on her face, shoulders tight.

"We only have one room," she told him over her shoulder.

"I'm sorry, Ms. Ambrose," the apologetic clerk said. "But this was what was booked for you. It's a very nice room, overlooking the dolphin-swim area."

"I'm sure it's lovely, but we need two rooms."

He was going to keep his mouth shut tight, because he didn't particularly have a problem with sharing a room. In fact, he preferred it. He wasn't used to having privacy, being alone. He had thought when he got back to the States that he would crave that space, and for the first few weeks, it had been blissful. But then it had gotten lonely. The downside of privacy was having no one to talk to, no one to share a thought or crack a joke with. He'd been in an all-male unit, and he missed the camaraderie, though not the smell. It had been a long time since he'd been allowed or able to share a space with a woman and all her feminine scents and quirks.

Even if he and Melanie weren't being intimate sexually, he wanted to be in her presence for a couple of days. He wondered what it took to make her laugh on a regular day, a day when she hadn't just been dumped.

"We have an additional room available at the same package price as the first room," the clerk said.

Melanie blanched. "Oh. Well. Never mind." She glanced back at him. "I can call Ian. I mean, he should pay for your room. He's the one who wanted you here. I'm sorry, I already maxed out my credit card paying for the trip package. I can't afford another room."

Hold up. "*You* paid for the trip?" he asked, appalled. "What do you do for a living?" Not that it mattered. Ian made a ton of money, there was absolutely no reason he should have his girlfriend paying for his vacation. If they were both financially secure, sure, go halfsies, but Hunter was pretty goddamn sure that Melanie was not in the same income bracket.

"I'm a PR rep. It's a good job, but it's not enough to pay for two rooms in Cancún." There were suddenly tears in her eyes. "I'm sorry. This is all such a disaster. I have no idea why Ian would do this to me. I'm starting to think he actually hates me." Her bottom lip trembled. "I've never had anyone be downright mean to me before. What did I do to deserve this?"

Hunter opened his mouth to reassure her, but she just kept rolling.

"And I mean, this is so embarrassing. We're holding up the line and I don't know what to do." She turned back to the clerk. "I'm sorry. We'll just take the one room." Then her head swiveled again back to him. "Unless you want to pay for another room and bill Ian?"

"Uh, no. I can't afford another room either, and there's no guarantee Ian will pony up." He could barely afford his rent. "I think you're stuck with me. But no worries, I don't snore."

She gave him a wan smile, then turned back to the desk clerk. "Okay, I guess we'll make the best of it. I'm sorry for holding things up."

He smiled at her and assured her it was not a problem. Hunter scanned the lobby, getting the feel for the resort, and listened to the clerk tell Melanie about the buffets, the pool and how to book her excursions if she hadn't already. He was still just floored that Melanie had footed the bill. It made him more determined than ever to make sure she enjoyed her vacation. The lobby was open-air, and he had to admit, while he'd missed snow when he'd been deployed, he appreciated the warm air wafting over them from the ocean breeze. It smelled like salt water and relaxation.

When Melanie held up the key to show him, her lips pursed, he grabbed hold of both their suitcases and prepared to follow her. "I can sleep on the floor. I'm used to it."

But she paused in lifting her sunglasses to her face and said, "Melly Ambrosia wouldn't worry about sharing a king-size bed with her bodyguard. She wouldn't think twice about it. So I'm okay with it if you are. No reason you should have to suffer because Ian is a jerkface. I promise I won't kick you, and I don't travel in my sleep."

Fair enough. "If you're sure you don't mind. I can't say I'll turn down a mattress over the floor."

He felt even more strongly about it when they reached the room and saw the wall-to-wall ceramic tile. That would hurt to sleep on, no doubt about it. She realized it, too.

"Uh, yeah, we can share the bed." She tossed her purse onto the surface in question. "Jeez, frickin' Louise, this is ridiculous! I want to strangle that man. Here we are in Cancún, two total strangers sharing a room, and why? Just why exactly?" She hauled her suitcase over to the luggage rack and viciously unzipped it. "I don't know. That's the answer to that question. I. Don't. Know."

She was fully entitled to have a meltdown, and frankly, she was showing a lot more restraint than he would have under the circumstances. "Maybe you should call Ian."

"I don't have an international data plan, and I'm not wasting another dime on that man."

He couldn't blame her for that. "Then screw Ian Bainbridge. You can pepper him with questions when you get back. But right now, let's bust open the complimentary minibar and check out the veranda. Dolphin view, remember?" He had no idea what that meant, exactly, but clearly it was something she'd chosen when she'd booked the room.

Melanie took a deep breath and released it. "You're right. You're totally right." She yanked off the sweater she was wearing, revealing a tank top underneath. "I'm burning up."

So was he. He kicked off his dress shoes and unzipped his bag to find his sandals. "Feels good, doesn't it? We're supposed to get a blizzard in Chicago in two days, so you can take a bunch of beach selfies and post them online to make your friends jealous."

Sitting on the edge of the bed, he took his socks off and wiggled his toes. He was unbuttoning his shirt when Melanie turned to respond to him. Her mouth fell open, then she quickly clapped it shut. "What?" he asked.

"Nothing."

"Should I go into the bathroom to change my shirt?" He didn't see the point, but it was her hotel room. She'd paid for it. He was still the employee, technically.

"No. Of course not. I mean, you're going to be at the beach with me. I can handle seeing your chest."

She sounded flustered. She looked flustered, running her hands through her hair.

That was promising.

But then she went over to the patio door and slid it open. "Oh! Hunter, there are dolphins out here!"

"On the veranda?" he asked, joking.

"No, you goof. In the water. Look."

He took his shirt and his undershirt off and dutifully walked over to the open doorway. On the veranda were a hammock and two chairs. Beyond the railing was some sort of grotto, and yep, there were a couple of dolphins cruising around, doing what dolphins do.

"Very nice."

"Aren't they cute?" She moved across the patio and leaned over to take a closer look. Her bottom lifted up toward him in those tight jeans.

"Very cute." He was definitely appreciating the view.

"Why do they slap the water with their tails?"

"I don't know. But they must have a porpoise." He moved up next to her as he deadpanned the worst pun ever.

"What?" She glanced over at him, her lips moving as she silently repeated what he had just said. "Oh, my

God. Really? For a guy who looks so serious all the time, you crack an awful lot of jokes."

"I'm multilayered." Actually, it was a coping mechanism. The shrink he'd been ordered to see after his injury had told him that. It seemed to be working just fine for him, so he wasn't going to bother making any changes.

"Why did you become a bodyguard?"

"Because I'm not qualified to do anything else."

"Is that the only reason?"

He hesitated, resting his forearms on the railing and staring down at the rippling water. The dolphins were making clicking sounds in the background, and somewhere on the other side of the resort mariachi music was playing. "No. I wanted to protect people. Do something useful. Leaving the military made me feel as though I didn't have a purpose anymore."

"I can see that about you," she said quietly. "So you think you'll keep doing this line of work? Do you work for a firm?"

"Yes. I'm not good at paperwork." It was true. He preferred action, and he hadn't wanted to be bothered with starting up his own business or doing consulting work. It was easier to sign on with a security firm and be out in the field. He had expected it would give him the adrenaline rush he had experienced in the Marine Corps, but he had learned that the work was mostly monotonous.

The other thing he had discovered was that it opened him up to conversations with his clients. Or mostly, it opened him up to them telling him about their lives, while he played the listener the way he always had. His mother had always told him he had a face that made people confess all their sins, and honestly, he had no clue why. Maybe his silence was the only invitation they needed. Plus he didn't judge. "It's not what I expected," he said honestly. "I was looking for more action."

"I'm sort of a bummer of a client, then, aren't I? You aren't going to see much action with me. Zero action here."

She had no idea what that particular phrasing did to him. It was a good thing only the dolphins could see that he was tenting his dress pants. "You never know. Sometimes there's action when you least expect it."

The dolphin snorted from his blowhole.

Damn right.

4

Melanie would swear she could smell Hunter's skin. The sun was heating up his bare chest and arms, and he smelled earthy and raw, like a man. She had been trying desperately not to look at his chest, but she had failed miserably. She kept peeking over at him every thirty seconds or so. He looked even better than her imagination could have prepared her for. All hard and muscular and somehow not pasty white like she was, but golden, with a sprinkling of chest hair.

"I'm starving," she blurted. "Can we go get a late lunch?" With all the movement of the day, the one thing she'd never done was eat. She was starting to feel light-headed, and it was only partially because Hunter was a hottie with his shirt off.

"Of course. We're on your schedule, remember?"

She remembered, but it made her uncomfortable. She'd never had an employee in her life. She had always been the one taking orders, not giving them. It felt awkward to say the least. "Okay. I don't need to change. I just want to grab something quick, like at the buffet. Then go to the pool. I'll save the beach for the day after tomorrow." She straightened up and moved back toward the door. "Tomorrow I scheduled the horseback riding. Are you sure you want to do that with me?"

"I'm doing it. Melly needs a bodyguard. I'm that guy."

Of course. He was right on her heels. "You don't have to, you know. I'm happy to let you off the hook, tell Ian you did your job and let him pay the bill. He deserves it."

"But what if you really are in danger?" Hunter walked over to his suitcase and pulled out a T-shirt.

"I'm not in danger. If Savannah the Stalker was smart enough to figure out I was dating Ian when it was a secret, she's smart enough to figure out he dumped me. I'm on a trip to Mexico without him—that should speak volumes." She rooted around in her purse for some sunscreen and started slapping it on her face. Every time she talked about Ian, she got annoyed. "She is a pretty dedicated stalker, but seemingly nonviolent. She fancies herself in love with him."

"I'd feel better just doing my job. What if she sees you as competition?"

"Why would she wait until after Ian dumped me to attack me, and a billion miles from home to boot? It's totally illogical."

"You may have a point. But just humor me, please."

"Fine. But can we make a pact to not mention Ian or stalkers anymore? Unless it's absolutely necessary? I'm over it."

"I can tell." He gave her a searching look. It was… sympathy.

That was the last thing on God's green earth she wanted. A hot bodyguard feeling sorry for her. She was tempted to toss the bottle of sunscreen at him, but resisted. Not the kind to take her frustration out on the wrong person, she just zipped her lips and rubbed the lotion into her skin. "You know, you don't have to look at me like that. Like the pathetic loser that you're stuck with."

"Hey, I'm sorry." He gave her a different expression, as if he was purposefully trying to lighten the mood. "No sympathy here. None whatsoever. I just don't know if I'm supposed to talk about it with you or not. You need a signal to let me know if I'm supposed to comment or not when you bring it up. I need a cue card."

"Ha-ha." From his point of view, she could see that he was standing in figurative quicksand, and the way he'd switched gears so easily made her relax a little. She could tell he was trying to make this whole debacle easier on her. "Okay, how about this?" She made an X with her arms over her chest. "I'll just give you the universal sign for the buzzer when I catch myself talking about the thing I don't want to talk about and don't want you continuing to talk about it."

His eyebrows shot up. "Will you please just get drunk and cry like everyone else on the day of a breakup?"

She laughed. "I already did that. Well, the crying. Shockingly, the vodka didn't even give me a buzz."

"Let's fix that."

Then he took his pants off.

What the…? Melanie gaped at him. He was just standing there casually in his tight boxer briefs, rooting around in his bag.

Her mouth watered. His butt was firm. She'd never seen a butt like that. "What are we fixing?" she asked, thoroughly confused. Her thoughts were scattered, and it had to be from lack of food. Not because she was three feet away from a six-foot-one muscle man in his underwear who she wasn't allowed to touch.

Right? She wasn't allowed to touch? Hunter certainly looked touchable, in all kinds of places. Touchable and suckable and…

He laughed. "Let's feed you."

Melanie felt her cheeks burn. She was ogling him. Just flat-out consuming him with her eyes, which was so out of line on every level. "Great, thanks. You might need pants, then." The minute the words were out of her mouth, she wanted to retract them. She shouldn't be mentioning his lack of pants. She should be channeling Melly Ambrosia and be casually unconcerned with his state of undress. He was going to think she was neurotic and undersexed.

It was the truth, but he didn't need to know that any more than he already did.

"I'm working on it." He unfurled a pair of cargo shorts that had been rolled up into the size of a cannoli.

It was a welcome distraction. "Your packing skills are impressive."

"Military talent." He pulled on his shorts.

The bend gave her an even better view of all that he had to offer. She looked away, feeling guilty for objectifying her bodyguard. Then looked again.

She was hopeless. But she'd never been confronted with the reality of a hot man before. "I can tie a cherry stem with my tongue," she said. "That's my only talent."

"Only talent?" His eyes darkened. "Somehow I doubt that."

If air could crackle, the space between them would be doing it. If she didn't know better, she'd almost think that Hunter was attracted to her. But maybe she was just projecting. "I suppose I have another talent or two. I can fit a whole banana in my mouth at once."

Hunter's fingers paused in the middle of zipping up his shorts. "Are you kidding me?"

"No." She shook her head, realizing she sounded not only flirty, but downright dirty. That was a total accident. She really could deep throat a banana, but what was funny and cool at eight sounded utterly wrong at twenty-eight. "That sounds kind of sexual, though, doesn't it? I didn't mean it like that. Jeez, I need carbs."

"Screw the carbs. I'm getting you a banana." He shook his head. "Damn. That's a visual I won't be able to shake."

Great. "Too freak show?" she asked, tucking their room key into her front pocket.

"Too sexy." He stepped into his sandals. "Or did you forget that we have to share this bed tonight?"

Oh, she hadn't forgotten. The last thing she could possibly do was forget that they would be sharing a bed. Granted, it was king-size. They could probably slide one of those dolphins into bed between them, it was so roomy, but nonetheless, it was just one bed. Under the covers. Together. Her and Marine Man and all his two thousand body parts.

"I'm sorry. Should I sleep on the floor, then?" Now, why in the hell did she say that?

"Why in the hell would you say that?" Hunter asked. "What kind of an asshole do you think I am that I would let you sleep on the tile floor while I take the king-size bed?" He was scowling at her, yanking open the door to the hallway so hard, it slammed into the wall.

"I didn't mean to suggest you're an asshole. I'm just embarrassed because I told you my only talent is deep throating." Poor choice of wording. Her cheeks burned and her mouth went hot. She needed some protein. And carbs. And sugar. Anything to put in her mouth so she would stop talking.

Hunter groaned. "Oh, my God. I'm fighting to stay professional here."

Wait just a minute. "I saw you in your underwear!" Did that constitute professionalism in his book? It did not in hers. She'd never once gone into Bainbridge Studios in her bra and panties. Though she had been diddling the boss on occasion. Huh. Maybe she didn't have a leg to stand on.

They started down the hallway toward the large main restaurant that served an all-day buffet.

"Fair enough. Should I stop changing in front of you?"

As if. "No, of course not. I want you to feel comfortable."

They looked at each other and started laughing. "This is weird," she told him, amused.

"It's been an odd day," he agreed.

It had been. Hunter had woken up expecting the perk of leaving the deep-freeze weather behind, but not much else. Instead, he'd gotten Melanie, who was the most intriguing mix of uptight and sensual that he'd ever encountered. She didn't seem to recognize how attractive she was, and she certainly didn't know how much she was turning him on.

He didn't think he was doing a great job of hiding

it, but she was totally blind to his desire to push her against the nearest wall and kiss her senseless. But he'd live with the sexual frustration for now and feel her out a little further. In the restaurant he loaded up a full plate of food, then realized he couldn't juggle it and his drink at the same time. His arm was throbbing from hauling the luggage around. The doctor had told him he should expect to have pain for upward of six months, and he hadn't been kidding. Three months in, it still hurt like a mother when he was least expecting it.

Melanie was sitting at the table they'd been shown. He deposited his plate and asked her if she needed a drink.

"Maybe it's time for a fruity drink like a rumrunner."

"I don't think they have those in here, but I can go to the bar."

"Oh, no, never mind." She waved her hand. "Sit down. I asked the waiter to bring us soft drinks. Is a regular cola okay?"

"Sure, that's great. Thanks." He joined her, sipping the ice water already on the table. "So have you been here before?" he asked.

"I've never been to Cancún, no. In fact, I've never been to Mexico." She glanced around. "I like this inclusive package so far. It's great not to have to worry about paying a bill or a tab. I grew up in a normal middle-class family, but we didn't do vacations like this."

"I didn't, either. It was just me and my mom, and it was an expense she couldn't afford. My father died in combat."

Her face grew sympathetic. "I'm sorry."

"Thank you." He didn't say, "it's okay," because it

hadn't been. Not for his mother; not for him. But he'd dealt with it as a kid the best way he'd known how. "I was six years old, and I became the man of the house, in my eyes. Mom worked really hard as a waitress. Her hours were rough, but we made it work."

"It doesn't surprise me then that you grew up wanting to protect people. You started out wanting to take care of your mother."

He studied her as she ate a burrito with a fork, thinking about what she'd said. "I guess to a certain extent, yes. But don't give me too much credit. I was a little shit often enough to drive my mom crazy. How about you? I doubt you were a troublemaker."

"Why do you keep assuming I'm such a good girl?" she asked, looking exasperated.

There was something so forthright and honest about Melanie. He couldn't imagine her doing something devilish as a little girl. He couldn't help but smile. "Just a feeling I have. It's not a criticism. There's nothing to brag about in being a brat."

"I'm not boring," she added, sounding mulish.

"No one said you were. I don't find you boring." He found her arousing, intriguing, sexy as hell. And sweet. There was something really revealing about the way she was handling Ian's dickish move of that morning. She was showing a normal range of emotions, but she wasn't ranting or screaming or crying in a way that was beyond reason. She was classy. While his mom was an amazing lady, she was also loud and brassy, and a fighter. She had thrown a brick at her boyfriend's car when she'd discovered him cheating when Hunter was in middle school, and he had backed her up on it. Melanie didn't seem like that type of woman at all.

"I find you fascinating," he told her honestly. "I'm not sure why you're not sending Bainbridge a slew of nasty text messages."

"How do you know I'm not?"

"You haven't touched your phone. I'm trained to notice these things, remember?"

"Do you ever get distracted?" she asked, tilting her head. She picked up the soft drink the waiter had brought for her and delicately flicked her tongue over the tip of the straw.

Uh, yes. He watched her slide her tongue seductively along that piece of plastic, like she might do to his cock under the right circumstances. "You're changing the subject," he told her. "And you can suck that straw all you want right before tying off a cherry and deep throating a banana, but I'm still going to press you about Ian. I just want to make sure you're okay."

She made a face and set the drink down. Then she put her arms up in an X. "Nah. This is one of those times."

He'd brought that one on himself. "Smart-ass."

"Nope. I'm a good girl, remember?"

Hunter chewed his food and swallowed, washing it down with some water. He was ready for a beer, though he wasn't going to have one since he was still on duty. "I do think you're a good girl. But there's a little bit of Melly in you, isn't there?"

"I don't know," she said ruefully. "If there is, she never gets to come out."

"Here's your chance." So maybe that was self-serving. Maybe that was him being masochistic. Because if Melanie holding back had him this hard, he couldn't even imagine how dangerous she would be in her free-spirited porn-star persona.

But he was sure in the hell willing to try.

Melanie picked up her straw. Without saying a word, she made it disappear almost entirely into her mouth and throat.

Holy crap. Melanie had skills that he would like to have used on him. Repeatedly. He felt his eyebrows rise. Her hair was disheveled and her cheeks pink. The top of her chest was pink, too, whether from being overheated or from arousal, he didn't know. He did know that she looked amazing, like someone he would like to find underneath him, naked and writhing. There was something about the look in her eye…

"That's not Melly. That's all you, Melanie. And you're goddamn gorgeous."

5

MELANIE COULDN'T BELIEVE she had just taken her straw deep in front of Hunter. What the hell was wrong with her? That was not appropriate by any stretch of the imagination, but what had being appropriate ever gotten her?

On vacation with a total stranger, that was what.

"Thanks," she said, after removing the straw. Her first instinct was to demur, or point out her flaws. But there was genuine appreciation on Hunter's face, and she decided just to sit back and accept the compliment, and not wonder about its sincerity. "Sometimes I surprise even myself."

The food was working its magic, and she actually felt human again. It had been a hell of a day.

Hunter leaned across the table. "So now I know all I need to do is call you a good girl and you'll show me your naughty side."

He was flirting, he really was. There was no denying that tone. He'd even shifted closer to her.

"I don't think I'm that easy," she said, matching her tone to his. Her voice lowered, she leaned, as well.

"I didn't mean to imply you were. But you're on vacation. You should feel free to relax a little. Or a lot, depending on your mood."

"I feel much better already." She glanced at his plate. "Are you done? Should we go to the pool?" Seeing Hunter in trunks would be anticlimactic after his underwear, but she relished the idea of lying in a chaise longue and enjoying the view.

"Sure." He politely waited for her to stand up, then gestured for her to walk ahead.

There was something to be said for gentlemanly behavior. Melanie realized she hadn't noticed its absence, but even simple gestures like Hunter opening the door for her were appreciated and noteworthy. That was sad. It was a prime example of how low her expectations of men had become. When had that happened? In her quest to be a contemporary and independent woman, had she allowed men to slack off on basic courtesies? Clearly the answer to that was yes.

Maybe Hunter was doing it because he was a hired gun, but she didn't think so. It just seemed part of his nature, fresh and genuine.

She was grateful for the way he had been treating her. He'd let her lay her head in his lap; he'd made her laugh. Listened to her bitch about Ian. He hadn't had to do any of that. Funny to think that in her quest to find men she'd thought were creative, artistic and therefore exciting, she'd probably passed up a guy or two like Hunter. Manly, sexy, gentlemanly.

Maybe it wasn't too late to learn the lesson.

Maybe she could strike up a friendship of sorts with Hunter while they were here in Cancún together and she could feel out what it would be like to spend time with a guy like him. It might help her relax and be more open to dating a variety of men in the future, instead of homing in on a specific type.

"I can't even imagine what it was like to be deployed," she said, making conversation. Asking about a huge chunk of his adult life seemed a good way to make him open up. "It must have been really hard."

They were walking along the path toward their room, and Melanie lifted her face to the warm sun.

Hunter shrugged. "It was a job. I did it. I came home."

Well, that was revealing. "Thanks for sharing," she told him ruefully.

"What am I supposed to say?"

"I don't know. A story, your feelings. I'm just trying to get to know you a little better."

"I don't do feelings. Ask my ex-girlfriend."

"But you're not insensitive or a brute or anything." She knew he wasn't. He'd already displayed a great deal of compassion for her.

"I don't think so, no. I can talk about your feelings. Just not mine."

"I don't want to talk about my feelings."

"Then we're on the same page. Let's talk about bananas and cherries and porn-star names again." He reached out and took her arm, shifting her out of the way of a giant lizard a foot to her right.

She felt her eyeballs bulge. "What is that?" she gasped.

"I don't know. I doubt it's dangerous, but you probably shouldn't step on it."

"Yuck." She shuddered and moved closer to Hunter. "I think we've exhausted the porn-star-names conversation. Let's talk about movies or music or something instead."

"We could just go swimming and not talk at all."

Nice. There was a big hint. "Are you saying I'm annoying you?"

"No. I just think that maybe you need to stop thinking so much and just do, you know what I'm saying?"

"No. I'm doing right now, aren't I? And since when is talking thinking?"

His hand was still on the small of her back, big and warm. "I don't believe you can talk without thinking."

"You technically can't swim without thinking, either. In fact, you can't do anything without thinking."

"But do you have to think so hard?"

Starting to feel criticized, she glanced up at him. "What exactly is your objection to thinking?"

He hesitated. "Would it sound completely bizarre if I said I just want you to enjoy yourself? That I feel bad that you're here on your own dime and I want this to be a decent memory, not one you always look back on with total regret?"

She was touched. Genuinely. His expression showed that he meant it, but that it pained him to say it out loud. "Thanks. I can see that nearly killed you to say. How about we strike a deal? I will enjoy myself, and you'll allow yourself to occasionally have feelings. Sound good?"

The corner of his mouth turned up. "Do I have to talk about them out loud?"

"Only if you want to. But you can express them nonverbally if you'd like."

"You don't even know what I want to express nonverbally right now. It would probably scare you."

"Are you going to punch me?"

"What?" He looked shocked. "No, of course not."

"Then why would I be scared?" She was hoping that he meant what she thought he meant. Something that involved him leaning over and kissing her.

He gave her a slow, devastating smile that went straight to her inner thighs. "I guess you wouldn't be." They had both stopped walking, and he turned completely to her. "You're very complex, aren't you?"

"I'm a people pleaser," she told him truthfully. "Pragmatic, organized."

"Yet secretly you're a romantic."

She was. She hadn't had much opportunity, but she had her moments of gushing and sighing over True Love and the overblown gestures that could accompany it. Putting her hands up in an X, she said, "If you're not going to talk about your feelings, I'm not going to talk about mine."

"You said I can show mine nonverbally."

"And you said I wouldn't want to know what you were thinking."

He stepped closer to her, and she stood her ground, even though she was flustered, curious about what he would do. He brushed his thumb across her bottom lip, causing her to shudder, a deep ache springing up inside her.

"I'm thinking that if you're not in danger, then there is no reason we can't have a little fun together."

Okay, so maybe he was attracted to her. That impression had been growing all day, and now there was no mistaking it. "What kind of fun?" she breathed, because she wanted to hear him say it out loud.

His eyes were dark with desire, and she could smell him and all his manly man perfection. "Naked fun."

"Oh." She swallowed hard. She wanted to. She really did. But she needed to think about it. She wasn't one to dive into anything, least of all a man's pants. If she slept with Hunter and it was disastrous, then she was stuck with him for six more days. She wasn't on her A game. She needed a good night's sleep and a list of pros and cons before she got naked. He was different from her usual bed partner, and frankly, she was feeling a touch insecure given how little desire Ian had had to tear up the sheets on a regular basis.

"I don't think… I mean, Ian and I just broke up. Er, he just broke up with me. I don't think I would be very fun in bed. Not tonight anyway." His expression was completely unchanged. No reaction whatsoever as she spoke. Suddenly, she felt as if she was the biggest idiot in the world. Here a totally hot bodyguard was saying he wanted to have sex with her, and she was shying away from him? So she added, to keep the door open for later, "Maybe later this week?"

HUNTER CONTINUED TO stare at Melanie for a minute, not sure he was hearing her right. Was she freaking kidding? She was saying no, she did not want to have sex with him, but maybe she might be able to pencil him in for a bang later in the week? Who did that?

He got it. She was just hours out of a relationship. Maybe it was too soon to sleep with someone without it resulting in severe awkwardness. But she could at least let him kiss her before she decided. And throwing him a pity promise? She could keep it. Screw that. He didn't want her sleeping with him because she didn't know how to say no.

"Don't do that," he told her, sounding rougher than he intended. "Tell a man yes or no, never maybe. Know what you want."

He was being brusque, but he heard her words and realized that was exactly how she had ended up being dumped by note card. She was right—she was a people pleaser. If he couldn't have sex with her, he could at least help her see her own worth. She didn't need to do anything just because a guy wanted her to.

Her eyes widened. "Then…no."

He nodded. "Fair enough." Stepping back, he created more space between them. He may not like her answer, but he was glad she'd stood up for herself. "Let's go swimming."

He should have kissed her. He should have made her want him first, before he'd thrown it out there that they should get naked. It had been an impulsive miscalculation on his part, and now all Hunter could think about was Melanie naked and how he would never get to see it.

She had changed into a bikini, but she was wearing a giant white cover-up over it. She had pulled her hair into a ponytail and was sporting sunglasses so that he couldn't see her eyes. She had been almost completely silent since she had rejected him, which was unnerving. If there was one thing he'd learned about Melanie in the course of only one day, it was that she liked to talk. But now she was sitting at the pool on a lounge chair, idly flipping through a magazine. He was on his phone, searching the internet for Bainbridge's photography.

Hunter wasn't going to see Melanie naked or even

in a bathing suit, since she was covered from knee to neck as thoroughly as a nun. So bored, frustrated and curious, he was stooping to the level of stalking her online. So far all he'd found was tiny shots of the nude series, and he couldn't in any way distinguish the individuals in the picture, even when he enlarged it.

He would have expected Ian to check in with him, but he hadn't. Hunter suspected that Melanie was right—there was no danger whatsoever. Ian had contracted him for a week just to have a built-in story to get Melanie on the plane. Which was the ultimate in cruel breakups. Hunter hoped the guy's business tanked and he developed a painful rash on his balls. Melanie didn't deserve to be treated like that.

Of course, Hunter had been something of a jerk himself, coming on too strong. She was mourning a lost relationship and he'd been all "hey, let's get it on." Smooth. But he'd spent the majority of his adult life with guys. What did he know about romance?

Nothing. A whole lot of nothing.

One photograph was more promising than the others. The crowd was smaller, and the individuals more spread out. The subjects were in and around a tree. Enlarging the photo, he saw Melanie immediately. Then was sorry he had. She was wearing panties and body paint and glasses, but nothing else. Her body was exactly as he'd imagined it—curvy and luscious with a nipped-in waist and perfect breasts. His mouth started to water, especially given the secret smile she was wearing, as if she was aware of how naughty she was being. It was a smile from one lover to another, and he wished it were directed at him.

She was painted brown, to look like bark, but his

thoughts turned to chocolate and how he could drizzle it over her nipples and lick it off her, one teasing flicker at a time. Shifting in his beach chair, he drew his knees up to hide the fact that he was sporting a giant hard-on. Man, it had been such a long time since he'd buried himself in a woman.

"I'm going swimming," he announced. The cold water would shrink his dick up soon enough. He'd keep an eye on Melanie from the pool.

She lowered her magazine. "Is the water cold?"

"I don't know. I haven't gone in yet."

She made a face at him. "Well, report back."

He thought about suggesting she get up and stick a toe in to find out for herself, but she'd probably throw her magazine at him. Melanie was in a mood, one he didn't entirely understand. Was it him and his ill-timed come-on or was it Ian and his jerk move? No clue. So he just gave her a double thumbs-up. "I'm on it."

That brought a smile to her face. "You're not the double thumbs-up kind of guy."

"What kind of guy am I?"

She hesitated. But then she said, "Dangerous."

Hunter stood at her feet. "Good dangerous or bad dangerous?"

"Good dangerous. Sexy, not scary." Melanie sat up and tossed her magazine down. "Maybe I'll go in with you."

Progress. Thinking he was sexy was a definite step in the right direction. She might not be willing to sleep with him, but at least he could freely ogle her. When she stood up, she peeled off her cover-up and revealed a perfect body in a red bikini. His breath caught.

When they got to the pool edge, Hunter sat down

and dropped his feet in. It wasn't bathwater, but it wasn't frigid, either. It was a good temperature. He cupped some water in his hands, and without turning around hurled it at Melanie.

She squealed, then made little huffing sounds. Grinning, he turned to see her wiping water off her chest. Yes. Direct hit. "How is it?"

"It's cold, jerk face."

"It is not."

"Then, splash yourself with it."

"I will."

As she gingerly eased herself down onto the concrete next to him, he splashed water over his arms and chest. It was refreshing.

Without warning she tried to push him in, but he had anticipated the move, and she wasn't strong enough to budge him more than an inch. He quickly regained his balance and flashed her a smile. "Seriously? That's your best?"

She was pursing her lips. "Damn it. I had visions of you tumbling in face-first and me laughing."

"I can take a dive if it will make you happy."

Melanie laughed. "No. That's not the same thing."

"You sure?" He made as if he was going to fall in. "Whoa. Whoa. Uh-oh." The water he'd splashed on her had given her goose bumps and tight nipples. Her skin brushed against his, cool and smooth. "I'm going to fall. Help."

She shook her head and rolled her eyes. But then she placed her hand on his back and shoved. He arched his back and fell in, enjoying the cold water and the soundlessness of being completely submerged. When he came up, she was smiling at him. He went back under and yanked her feet, not hard enough to pull her in, which might scrape her skin or knock her unconscious, but enough to startle her.

He shifted her feet apart so when he reemerged, he was between her legs and very close to both her belly and the tiny triangle of fabric covering her lady parts. Lady parts he wanted to explore quite thoroughly.

Her laughter died, and she looked down at him with censure, her hands dropping onto his shoulders. "This is not right, Hunter." But she didn't push him away.

"What? I'm cold. Your legs are warming me up."

"You're ridiculous."

"I have to be close to you to protect you." He gave her a wink.

"Now you're just being a tool."

But she still didn't shove him away.

Someone bumped into Melanie's shoulder as he was walking past. He glanced down at Melanie, then Hunter, then back to Melanie. "Do I know you?" he asked, tilting his head.

"She's a famous porn star," Hunter told him with a straight face. "You've probably seen her online."

The guy's expression lit up. "That's it!" He grinned and nodded. "All right, cool, nice to see you in person. Love your work, if you know what I mean." He waved and kept going.

Melanie glanced down at Hunter and said, "Seriously?" But she burst out laughing.

"You're famous. What can I say? Don't hide your light under a bush." He wasn't sure that was how the expression went, but he rolled with it.

"Why do I feel as though you're always saying

something perverted without actually saying something perverted?"

"Because I have mad skills." He stared at her belly button and the droplet of water that was rolling down over her flesh. He wanted to lick her, taste her. Slide his tongue into her belly button and right on down, taking a nip at the front of her bikini bottoms. "Why are you so gorgeous?" he murmured. "You're making this really difficult."

He looked up to find she was staring down at him, eyes wide, mouth open. She looked as if she wanted exactly what he wanted. For him to peel down her panties and use his tongue until she came hard, begging for more. Her legs had clamped onto his sides, her fingernails digging into his shoulders.

"I'm not trying to be difficult. I'm trying to avoid making a mistake."

"I respect that. Doesn't make me any less turned on. But I won't push you."

Even though it gave his arm a serious twinge, he lifted her down carefully into the water, onto his hips. She protested with a squawk but didn't resist beyond that. For a brief moment, he lowered them both and enjoyed the torturous feeling of her body all up on top of his, her ass nestled on his thighs and cock, her breasts pushing against his chest..

Then he tossed her fully into the water.

6

MELANIE SURFACED, HAIR in her face, water up her nose, snuffling and gasping and blind. Swiping at her eyes, she tried to open them so she could find Hunter and kill him. But it burned, so she wiped again and said, "That was mean!"

Especially since she had been seriously entertaining the idea of kissing him. He was so sexy and hard. And sexy. And hard. She had felt his erection nudging her in the most dangerous of places. Everything in her had felt hot and melting, despite her lower half being submerged in the water.

She no longer felt hot. She felt drowned.

Treading water, she finally pried her eyes open and glared at him. "What was that for?"

"I was distracting us both." He bobbed in the water and looked all kinds of nonchalant and gorgeous. "So I don't do something you'll regret."

"And you wouldn't regret it?" Damn it, why did she say that? Dipping her head back so she could slick her hair off her face, she floated up onto her back for a minute. When she straightened again she realized he was staring at her chest.

"No. I am one hundred percent certain I wouldn't regret a damn thing."

She felt her cheeks flush.

His gaze lifted, and he met her eyes with his. "But then again, I live my life forward, not backward. If I'm not hurting anyone, what's to regret?"

"Why did you and your girlfriend break up?" she asked. Sure, he'd said it was because he didn't express emotion, but what did that mean exactly? There had to be more to it than that.

He put his arms up in an X. "Nope. Not talking about that."

How annoying. He was throwing her veto rights back in her face. "Why? What do you have to hide?"

He shook his head. "Uh-uh. I'm not falling for that female manipulation. I have nothing to hide. I just don't see why we need to talk about my ex when what I really want to talk about is you."

That sounded just as manipulative as her question. "Maybe we should talk about the weather. It's a beautiful day."

"It is." He swam a little circle around her, as if he had a hard time standing still. "So how do you like your job?"

Her job made her think of Ian, of course. Without meaning to, she made a face.

He looked chagrined. "I'm sorry. That's probably a bad subject right now."

But she shook her head. "No, I have to think about it, deal with it. Everyone says don't get involved with your boss, and it turns out they're right." It made her feel glum. "I'm not ready to face being at work."

"You don't have to for another week."

"On the plus side, no one knew we were dating."

"Okay, this whole secret thing?" He held his palms out. "Bullshit. Complete and total bullshit."

"He didn't want it to compromise his work." It sounded lame even as she said it out loud. It was lame. "Plus he didn't want to incite his stalker."

"I don't get it. I can see wanting to keep you safe, but it's almost impossible to keep a stalker from ferreting out every detail of your life, and in the end all it did was insult you."

She had nothing to say to that. It just made her feel stupid. She had been stupid. Plain and simple.

When she didn't respond, he swore. "Shit. I'm sorry. I'm being insensitive. I'm just pissed on your behalf, Melly, that's all."

"I know." She did. Hunter wouldn't hide a relationship. He would think it was dishonest and disrespectful. She could already tell that about him. "And my name isn't Melly, you know." Melly was more fun than she was.

"You're Melly to me."

"A porn star?" She wasn't sure what would give him that impression of her since she'd turned down his overtures.

"No. Sexy but sweet. A good time but fiercely loyal. That's Melly. That's you."

Somehow it was exactly what she needed to hear. "Thanks, Hunter." But she still felt melancholy. "I'm sorry."

"Are you going to start apologizing for shit you don't have to apologize for? Because if you are, I'm heading to the hot tub instead."

"But..."

"But nothing."

He was right. She had nothing to be sorry about. So she'd made a poor choice in hanging in there with Ian. What of it? It wasn't the end of the world. It wasn't cancer or poverty or war. It wasn't even a waste of time necessarily because she had Learned Things. So really, why was she boo-hooing and taking on blame she shouldn't own?

So she just smiled at him. "You're right. I'm in Mexico, and back home there is three feet of snow on the ground. There is nothing to be sorry about."

"Damn straight." Hunter gestured to the swim-up bar. "Join me for a drink? It's on me."

She laughed. "It's all inclusive."

"Damn. I can't even look generous and dashing."

He had this ability to deliver lines with a completely straight face and a dry tone that if she didn't know him would have her wondering if he was kidding or not. But she saw through it. Forced circumstances allowed a quick assessment of someone else's character. He may look big and fierce and capable of snarling, but he was a softie at heart.

"You've been nothing but generous and dashing," she said, swimming next to him to the pool bar. "This is the oddest thing. I feel like a mermaid." She perched on a partially submerged concrete stool, most of her body still in the water, and leaned on the bar. "It must be really weird to be the bartender."

"Agreed. Do you care if I have a beer?"

"Why would I care?"

"Because I'm your bodyguard."

"Whatever." That was utter nonsense, and they both knew it. "Have a beer."

He sat on the stool next to hers, and for a while they sipped in companionable silence. Melanie wasn't always comfortable with conversational lulls, but this was different. It was a moment for just relaxing in the sun and having a fruity drink with a cocktail umbrella.

When she yawned and said she wanted to take a nap, Hunter readily went with her back to the lounge chairs. Melanie lay on her stomach on her towel with her head resting on her crossed arms. She closed her eyes. It was peaceful, soothing.

Until suddenly she felt Hunter's hand on her back.

"What are you doing?" She had almost been asleep.

"You're already starting to burn. I'm putting sunscreen on you."

She eyed him over her shoulder, trying to see if he had an ulterior motive, but he was just squirting sunscreen into his hands and working it into her flesh. Even with her sunglasses she could see he was right—her skin was pink. "Thanks."

It felt insanely good to have him massaging the lotion into her skin. He started from her shoulders and worked his way down, going under the string of her bikini top. She let out an involuntary groan. "God, that feels good."

"Your shoulders are really tense." He was squatting down next to her, so she could feel his body brushing against hers here and there. His voice was low, soothing.

Why didn't all men have voices like that? She felt safe, well cared for, when Hunter spoke. As if he could beat the crap out of someone who threatened her safety, yet could still touch her with care and tenderness. Not that he was being tender. He was being thoughtful, though. Or maybe it was just an excuse to arouse her and wiggle under her defenses. If that was the case, it was working. She felt relaxed and very much aware of how close his palms were to her backside. How easy it would be for him to slip his hands under the fabric and stroke her teasingly…

Clearing her throat, she clamped her thighs together. They were in public. She needed to get a grip. Plus she'd already told him she wasn't going to sleep with him. What kind of a flake would she look like if she changed her mind three hours later? Three days maybe wouldn't look so bad. Maybe by then she would feel a little more settled and confident.

She made eye contact with the woman a few feet to her right. The woman smiled, looking at her enviously.

"I wish my husband would massage me like that," the woman said. "You're very lucky."

"Oh, well," Melanie said for lack of anything better to say.

"Frank, see that?" The woman turned to her husband, who had an explosion of chest hair rising above a protruding belly. "Her husband is giving her a back rub."

Frank's eyebrows went up as he glanced over at them. "That's because his wife is hot."

The wife smacked Frank with her book, and justifiably so. Melanie gave an awkward laugh. "Oh, dear," she said, unsure what else to say. While Frank's wife was not twenty-five and a size two, she was an attractive sixty-year-old with a cute pixie haircut and a good figure.

"For what it's worth," Hunter said to the wife as

Frank heaved himself off his chair and lumbered to the pool, "I think Frank got the better end of the deal."

She smiled. "Thanks, that's sweet of you." Pointing her finger at Melanie, she said, "Hold on to this one."

"I'm not going anywhere," Hunter said mildly.

The melancholy she'd felt earlier came rushing back. She had been anticipating romance on this trip, and now she just felt...lonely. Hunter was better company than she could have imagined, and he was saving the vacation from being a complete disaster. But he wasn't hers. They weren't a couple. She wanted to be part of a couple with a guy like him, a man who was protective and attentive, but all she had was a breakup note and a bodyguard who might want to sleep with her, but nothing more.

It sucked. Just flat-out sucked.

But Hunter had magic hands, and between his touch and the sun's warmth she managed to doze off despite her sudden wistfulness.

She dreamed Hunter was making love to her while Ian stood in the background taking pictures. Even in her sleep it killed her arousal. They did not belong in the same dream. Period. Ian was her lackluster former reality. Hunter was her current fantasy.

HUNTER DEBATED LETTING Melanie sleep any longer. She probably needed the rest, but at the same time, she'd been out cold for forty-five minutes in the sun, and despite the sunscreen she was slowly baking to the color of watermelon innards. She hadn't reached lobster status, but she would if he didn't haul her Northern butt inside for the night. So he leaned over from his own chair and touched her shoulder.

"Melly, wake up, sweetheart." He wasn't sure when he had started thinking of her by her nickname or when exactly he'd earned the right to use a term of endearment, but it felt good to say it. Maybe he was craving female companionship more than he'd realized, and he didn't just mean the naked kind.

Her eyes opened slowly, and she looked disoriented. "Hmm?"

God, she looked sleepy and sexy, and he had an instaboner. "You're cooking like an egg out here. We should go inside for a bit."

"Oh." She lifted her head and tried to glance at her back, but just went cross-eyed in the process. "Okay. What time is it?"

"It's five. Actually, I guess the sun will be setting soon. I forget it's still winter when we're here in this kind of weather."

"Do they have bugs here?"

That seemed off topic. "There are bugs everywhere."

"I forgot the sun sets early, too. I didn't bring bug spray." She yawned and sat up. "I wonder if the gift shop has any."

"Let's wait and see if there are any mosquitos first." Though he didn't like how she worried all the time, he had to admit he liked that she was organized. Prepared. Being in the military had made him think in terms of readiness, and he appreciated that she was of a similar ilk. "You ready for dinner?"

"Can we get room service? I'm still really tired. I'm going to go to bed early tonight."

"Sure. No problem." Because what he needed was to be holed up in the room with blue balls. There wasn't even a table in their room, so it would be dinner in bed. Only what he wanted wasn't on the menu.

He helped her gather up her giant beach bag, though he was disappointed when she pulled her tent of a cover-up back on. Why women wore those things was beyond him. They were at a resort. It wasn't as though she was going to get bounced from the gift shop if she was in a bikini.

Back in the room, she pored over the room service menu for approximately a thousand years, asking frequent rhetorical questions.

"I wonder if the risotto is any good?"

"Do you think I can get the mushrooms separate or would it be premixed?"

"There's a soup of the day. I wonder if it will be vegetable based."

Finally, he couldn't take it anymore. "Why don't you call and ask?"

"Oh, I don't want to bother them."

He held his hand out for the book so that she no longer could abuse her viewing time. "Let me see." When she gave it to him, he glanced at it and said, "I want the sirloin."

"You didn't even look at anything!"

"I've seen all I need to." Beef, his mouth, they were good to go. "Make a decision, please. I'm hungry."

She took the book back and said, "I worry if I get a salad the lettuce might be wilty."

For hell's sake. There was absolutely no way to know any of the things she was pondering. There were greater risks in life than ordering a Cobb salad. "Then, don't get a salad."

Melanie was lounging on top of the bed in her bikini. The cover-up was off again because she'd said she was going to shower after they ordered room service. "Do you get grumpy when you're hungry? I'm sorry. I'll hurry up."

Being hungry wasn't helping, but his stomach wasn't the major issue. "No," he said shortly. "Now pick up the phone and order something."

"Okay. Jeez." She gave him a look as if she'd been chastised and picked up the phone.

Hunter went out onto the patio and got into the hammock. He didn't really want to be out here, but it was away from Melanie and all her sexiness. All he wanted to do was smack that sweet little ass of hers and get her moving. Then toss her down and make her forget about the goddamn risotto.

The dolphins were noisy, squeaking and splashing and slapping around. He wasn't sure if the pair was engaged in foreplay or having a marital spat. Or maybe it was two guys, and they were busy trying to show each other up. Whatever the situation, it wasn't exactly relaxing on top of his empty gut and his throbbing dick.

He wrestled himself out of the hammock and went back inside the hotel room, closing the slider door and locking it behind him. He closed the blinds.

"What are you doing?" Melanie asked, startled. She was rooting around in her suitcase.

"I'm just making sure you're safe in here. I'm going to go for a jog."

"Right now?"

She sounded so aghast he was amused. "Is there a better time?" He needed to work off some energy. He, too, went into his bag and pulled out his running shoes, shorts and a T-shirt.

"You said you were hungry. I ordered you food. It'll be cold when you get back."

"I don't mind. I won't be long." Just thirty minutes, that was all he needed. He just needed to run, to push himself past his sexual frustration. It was something he was good at.

But Melanie sounded huffy about the whole thing. "I can call them back and tell them to wait."

"You don't have to do that. I'll probably be back before they even get here. I just need to change."

He started toward the bathroom, but Melanie kept talking.

"Steak is tough when it gets cold."

How could someone so cute be so obtuse? He raised his eyebrows. "If you let me change, I'll be back in time."

"But I don't understand. Why right this minute?"

So she was going to make him spell it out. "Melly, watching you roll around on the bed was more than I could handle. I'm going to jog off my hard-on."

"I wasn't *rolling*." She glanced down at his jock. "Do you really have a... Oh."

"Yes, I do. Now can I go change?" So he could adjust and give himself some air. He was damn near on the verge of passing out from tight trunks.

"I think we should talk about this," she persisted.

That was it. If she wouldn't let him leave the room, he was changing right there. He yanked his trunks down and kicked them off across the tile.

Finally, there were no more questions. Just pure silence from Melanie.

He grinned as he bent down to retrieve his underwear from his bag.

7

MELANIE WAS SO shocked she almost fainted. She was utterly speechless. She might even have been drooling.

Why did she have to control everything? Why hadn't she just let Hunter go into the bathroom and change? Because now he was naked, and she couldn't look away. She was absolutely incapable of turning her head and giving him privacy. Not that he needed or wanted it. But she should. Because she should not be seeing Hunter like this, for reasons she could no longer remember.

Holy moly macaroni, the man was off the charts. He was hard. Everywhere. From neck to knee and beyond, with muscular thighs, ripped abs and an erection that was pointing skyward. When he turned to get his shorts out he obscured her view just slightly, but she was compensated by a profile shot of his ass. Which was a thing of perfection. A man shouldn't look that good. It just wasn't fair. Because it rendered seemingly intelligent women like herself speechless idiots.

"Enjoy your run," she finally managed, her throat tight. Her hands were making fists, so she forced herself to relax them, one finger at a time.

"Thanks. You know, maybe you're right." He turned back to face her.

Oh, no. Melanie tried to lock her gaze with his and keep her line of vision PG, but she couldn't stop herself. She glanced down again. That could all have been hers for the night. But like an idiot, she'd said no. "I don't think I've been right about anything," she said sincerely.

Hunter laughed. His penis bounced a little when he did. Damn it. How could he be hard like that? Just hard for no reason? And stay that way? She wondered what kind of lover he was. Serious, intense? Playful? Most likely all of the above.

"You're too hard on yourself," he told her. "I wish you'd just let go and trust your instincts instead of worrying about other people all the time."

"I'll work on that." She crossed her arms over her chest, very aware of her breasts and how her nipples had to be poking out of her bikini top. It was beyond her comprehension that he could just stand there naked and feel comfortable having a conversation with her.

He bent at the waist and pulled his underwear on. Finally. She gave an audible sigh. She wasn't cut out for this. Her life was orderly, well planned. This was all uncharted territory.

"Want to come for a run with me?"

The ridiculousness of that question jolted her out of her panic. "Please. I only run if someone is chasing me."

"I can chase you. In fact, I think I already am." He sat down to put on his shorts, followed by his socks and running shoes.

"Are you?" she asked, curious. Was he genuinely interested in having a fling with her, or had it been more of a spontaneous reaction to a convenient opportunity? Like when they passed out samples at the grocery store. You weren't hungry, but you took the sample anyway because it was being offered.

But Hunter nodded. "I am. I respect that you said no. But I'm attracted to you, and I'm not going to stop flirting with you. I'm optimistic things will go my way eventually. We have a whole week."

A whole week. Lord. "So what, marines always get their man, so to speak?"

"I think that's the Mounties. But when I want something, I put a lot of energy into getting it. And yes, I want you."

That put a tingle in places that hadn't tingled for weeks. She'd never had a man be so frank about his desire for her. In her experience most men were determined to display nonchalance. But Hunter clearly wasn't most men. She wasn't sure what to say to him. How to respond in an appropriate way. But then she remembered what he was telling her—go with instinct.

"I want you, too. That's not the issue." She let her arms drop down and took a deep breath and let it out slowly. No hiding. "I'm just not sure I'm ready to dive in to a vacation fling. I'm afraid I'll freak out and be disappointing."

He stared at her. She waited for him to speak. Any second now.

Seriously? She made herself vulnerable and told the truth, and he just stared at her?

"I like you," he said, finally. Simply. "If you are willing to get naked with me, how could I possibly be disappointed?"

"I don't know. I mean, men aren't exactly beating down my door to repeat the experience." *Okay, that was way too personal.* She mentally cringed. "Just forget it."

"No. I don't want to forget it." He came toward her, and she fought the urge to back up. "If they weren't satisfied, then they were doing something wrong. Not you."

"Maybe..." She wanted to believe that. She did, in her heart of hearts, truthfully. It was slow in coming, but she was realizing the issue was that she was choosing men poorly.

"No maybe, remember? Yes or no. In this case, the answer is yes."

Hunter cupped her cheek with his hand and studied her. He was waiting for permission to kiss her—she could see that. This was her choice. She wanted to. She did. She wanted to feel sexy and alive and desired, and she had no doubt Hunter would make her feel all of those things. Rocking slightly on her heels, she leaned up and in toward Hunter, intending to kiss him herself. A soft, exploratory kiss.

But he didn't wait. And it wasn't a tentative brush of his lips on hers. It was a possessive, full-on kiss with his mouth covering hers fully. He used her gasp of surprise to slip his tongue inside and tease her. It was hot, it was wet, it was an erotic dance that she hadn't been prepared for, and she gripped his arms, desperate to hold on. As they kissed, she felt the slow, languid heat build deep inside her, and she pressed into his touch, wanting more, wanting him.

Hunter broke away so suddenly, she stumbled forward. "I want to repeat that experience," he said, voice gruff. "I want to repeat it until you stop thinking and just feel."

That sounded like bliss. She wasn't sure she knew how to do it, though. "I think I'm willing to try."

"No think. Only yes or no."

Was he Yoda? Damn it. Let a girl waffle, what was so wrong with that?

She opened her mouth, but no sound came out.

Hunter turned. "I'll be back in twenty minutes."

"You're really leaving?" Why was she so pathetically bereft at the thought of being left alone? Because it had been the longest day in the history of long days. She was definitely lonely. And Hunter was filling that void for her. She quickly added, "Should I text you or something when the food arrives?"

"You don't have an international texting plan, remember? Don't worry about it. I won't be that long."

He wasn't gone long. But it gave her plenty of time to reflect on both that kiss and his body. She turned on the TV but everything was in Spanish, so it served poorly as a distraction. The food arrived, and she ate mechanically. She wasn't as hungry as she'd been at lunch. She was exhausted.

Everything had changed in the course of twelve hours. If anyone had told her when her alarm went off that morning she'd be making out with a bodyguard, she would have suggested they be committed. But now instead of thinking about Ian, all she could think about was Hunter. It seemed wrong.

Yet she couldn't stop herself.

Why exactly was it wrong? Ian had dumped her. She hadn't had sex in six weeks. She was lonely and wanted the ego stroke and an orgasm. People had rebound affairs all the time. She was on vacation and no one ever had to know.

After eating a third of her dinner, she decided she needed to take a shower. Despite Hunter's massage, she still had more knots in her shoulders than a pretzel factory. Leaving Hunter's steak covered on the tray on the bed, she stepped into the bathroom and into the shower, sighing in relief. She washed off the sunscreen, the anxiety sweat and hopefully the layer of insecurity she'd been wearing all day.

Hunter was right. Say yes or say no. It wasn't that hard.

By the time she reemerged wearing a tank top and shorts, her hair only towel dried, Hunter was back and his plate was empty. "Wow, you ate that fast."

"I'm efficient."

"I'm tired. Do you mind if I get into bed?"

"No, of course not." He pulled back one side for her. "I'm going to jump in the shower myself."

Melanie yawned. She would have thought she'd be out in thirty seconds flat, but instead she lay on the cool sheets, mind whirring. Her body was weary; her thoughts were not. She felt a bit as though she'd had too much coffee, and she couldn't hold on to a single train of thought. They rushed by like bullets, there and gone before she could grab one or dodge it.

She had the surreal feeling that she had imagined all of this, and that tomorrow she would wake up in her apartment in Chicago, freezing her butt off, with a good-morning text from Ian.

Then she realized suddenly and with startling clarity that, God, she hoped not.

She wanted to be right there, with Hunter. Not at home with Ian.

For once, just once, she wanted to do something not because it was logical but because it would feel good.

The answer was a yes.

HUNTER CAME OUT of the bathroom, clean but no less sexually frustrated. That kiss with Melanie had been hotter than even he'd been expecting. And he'd expected it to be smoking. What he hadn't anticipated was a five-alarm fire with barely any touching between them. If that was the beginning, he could only imagine the ending.

Melanie was under the covers on her back, looking at the ceiling. She didn't look anywhere near sleepy. "You okay?" he asked, towel around his waist.

She glanced over at him. "Yes."

"Are you sure?" She didn't look okay. She looked as if she was breathing heavily, her chest rising up and down unnaturally fast.

"Yes."

"Okay." He wasn't sure he believed her, but he wasn't going to force the issue.

"No, I mean *yes*." She rolled up onto her side, letting the sheet fall away from her.

She was not wearing a shirt. Or a bra. That was a glorious pair of breasts poking out from under the crisp white sheet. His mouth went dry. He froze in place.

"What..." Smooth. That was him. "I..." Even smoother.

Her hair was still damp from her shower, and it tumbled over her flesh in soft blond waves. Her cheeks were pink, the top of her collarbone stained as well from her anxiety, her arousal. She was gorgeous. Sexy as hell.

And she might be his tonight. He was a lucky bastard.

But something didn't feel right about this. He hesitated, waiting to be clear about what she was suggesting.

"What are you doing, Melly?" he asked, even as he stepped toward the bed, desperately wanting to pull that sheet all the way down and see what other surprises she had in store for him.

Melanie's cheeks grew pink. "Well, clearly I'm not doing it very well. I'm trying to let you know I want to—" her voice dropped to a whisper "—have sex with you."

That she was so clearly embarrassed made him feel guilty for pushing her to say yes or no definitively. Maybe she did want to have sex. But maybe she was just feeling raw and emotionally spent. He could be the kind of guy who would take advantage of the day from hell she'd had and get what he could out of it, or he could ease up, take it a little bit slow, see if it was really what she still wanted the next day.

"Is that right?" he asked. "And here I thought I was just your hired muscle." Wanting her to relax, he followed up his teasing words by leaning forward and kissing her softly on the lips. "I like this job, by the way. Best assignment I've ever had."

"Oh, yeah?" she whispered, breath tickling his lips. "You must be getting a decent paycheck."

"I'd do it for free." He brushed her hair off her face and cupped her cheek. As he leaned over her, he could smell the shampoo from her shower and see the pink freshness of her skin, the brightness in her eyes. She looked nervous but certain. Her fingers had risen to splay across his chest, and he found even that simple touch sexy as hell. "I'm glad to be here with you."

"I'm glad you are, too." She took his hand and squeezed it, then placed it squarely onto her breast.

Her flesh was warm, her nipple taut. "You sure about this?"

Melanie nodded. "Yes. I'm sure. I wanted this vacation to be a sex fest, and I have a very good feeling you can give me exactly that."

As his dick swelled, the knot holding his towel in place loosened. "Damn straight I can. You ready to get started?"

Just sex. Just a vacation get it on. That was exactly what he had been looking for, wanting. Melanie was hurt and confused from the unexpected ending to her relationship, so it was actually perfect timing for him. She wasn't going to have any unrealistic expectations. She would take comfort in being with him, and he would make her feel sexy. Which she was.

He would get some much-needed sexual satisfaction, and she would get an escape from the bad feelings of a breakup. Win-win.

"More than ready." She sat up, and the sheet fell to her waist. He'd seen her in a bikini, but aside from the beauty of her full breasts and tight pink nipples exposed to him, this view was completely different because she was offering herself to him intentionally. It was the hottest damn thing he'd ever seen.

When he got to the edge of the bed, her hand reached out, fingers shaking slightly, and loosened his towel. It fell with a soft thump onto the tile floor, and she sucked in her breath as she stared at him. He swelled even further at her scrutiny. When her hand closed around him, he was the one jerking air into his lungs on a low hiss. That tentative touch was almost more than he could bear.

He pressed her off him and down onto her back, climbing up next to her. She gave a soft cry of surprise. It was then he realized that she had laid out a row of condoms on the nightstand. She had been busy while he was in the shower. For a split second, he was disturbed by the thought that she'd brought those condoms with another man in mind, but he shoved that aside. Fuck Bainbridge. His loss that he wasn't here. He didn't deserve Melanie anyway.

Covering her body with his own, his hands on either side of her, Hunter bent down and kissed her softly. "Your lips are delicious. Soft and juicy."

"How can they be juicy?" she asked, arching up toward him when he drew back.

"They just are." He dipped down and sucked her bottom lip to taste her, to feel that soft give of her flesh beneath his.

Melanie gave a soft moan.

He cupped one breast, testing its weight, testing her reaction.

She sighed. "You know what really got to me earlier?" she asked.

"When I dropped my pants in front of you?" He nibbled at the corner of her mouth, wanting to take his time and explore all of her body, all of her reactions.

She giggled. "That tickles. And yes, that did get to me. But actually I was thinking about the massage you gave me. It both relaxed me and totally turned me on.

I was fantasizing about you slipping your finger into my bikini bottoms."

"What a coincidence. So was I." If they hadn't been in public he might have tested the waters.

But now they were blissfully in private, and Melanie had lost her shirt somewhere along the way. He wondered what was happening down south. "Roll over. I'll massage you again." Pushing back, he stood up and went back to the bathroom.

"Where are you going?"

She sounded upset that he was leaving, which was satisfying. "To get some lotion."

"Oh."

As he came back, squirting the scented lotion into his hand, he saw she had done as he'd told her to and rolled onto her stomach. She was resting her head on her hands and watching him with a small smile. "You don't have to do this, you know."

"Uh, yes, I do." He climbed back onto the bed. "This isn't a duty or charity on my part. I don't have to get my oil changed every three thousand miles. I don't have to show up at my friend Brent's annual clambake. This? I have to do this. For both of us." No one was going to sleep until there was at least one round of orgasms.

"No, I meant the massage. I sort of strong-armed you into it."

The woman needed to be spanked. She spent far too much time telling him what he shouldn't do for her. "You did not strong-arm me into it. You didn't even ask. Can I suggest something?" He started at her shoulders, enjoying the sigh of contentment she gave.

"What's that?"

"Zip it and let people do shit for you. Embrace your inner diva."

"I don't think I have one," she said so sincerely that he had to laugh.

"Well, let's go looking." Hunter settled himself over her, one knee on either side of her thighs. Her butt was still covered with the sheet, and he perched over her, their bodies just brushing occasionally as he kneaded the knots under her skin. Leaning forward, he kissed behind her ear, kissed her neck, kissed the side of her mouth that was available to him. "Are we close?"

"I don't think so," she murmured. Her eyes were closed, and he could feel her relaxing beneath him.

He moved on down her body, running his thumbs on either side of her spine. Her body was already familiar to him from his earlier massage, though now he had the luxury of moving farther and farther to either side until he was touching the swell of her breasts. She had a great chest that he was very much looking forward to enjoying thoroughly.

"Well, then, let's attack this from a different angle." He moved off her and slipped his hands lower, taking the sheet down with him. She was still wearing panties, which didn't surprise him. It had been daring enough of her to take her shirt off.

But he didn't hesitate to peel the panties down and off her ankles, exposing the curve of her backside to him. She sucked in her breath.

"Please don't massage me…there," she said.

"Why not?"

"It's weird."

Completely defying her, he cupped her cheeks with both hands and gently massaged her. It was a total turn-on, touching her while studying her body laid out for him. She looked so sexy, her lips swollen from his kisses, her hair wild and damp—but a little anxious.

She groaned even as she repeated, "This is weird."

"What's weird about it?" Hunter wiped his hands on the sheet to make sure there was no lotion remaining and lay down on his side next to her, feathering his palm across her backside.

"I don't know," she whispered, staring at him with limpid eyes. "No one has ever touched my butt before."

"You can't be serious." He stroked her flesh with a feathery touch, up and down, hoping she would relax. "If you try to tell me you're a virgin, I'm going to call you out on it because I don't believe you."

She rolled her eyes. "No, I'm not a virgin. What does that have to do with anything?"

"There is no possible way you can have sex without your butt being touched at some point." He kissed her before she could respond, teasing his tongue inside her mouth.

Melanie smiled and pulled away, sounding breathy as she spoke. "I meant the *way* you were touching it, kneading it like bread dough, not just any sort of general touching."

"That makes more sense. I stopped doing that. Should I stop doing this?" He reached around behind her and slipped his middle finger between her legs and into her moist heat, sliding in and out of her with a steady rhythm. She moaned softly and her hips rose involuntarily. Damn, that was sexy. She had the kind of body he loved. He'd lived in South Florida until he was ten years old and seen many beautiful Latina women in bikinis on the beach during his formative years. He appreciated curves on a woman, the classic hourglass with breasts and booty. With her tail end raised, he was getting more and more turned on. Melanie had a body built for sex.

He had a body built to satisfy her.

"No." She started to move onto his finger. "Please don't—"

"Please don't what?"

"Don't stop."

"Not until you tell me to," he promised. "Is this good enough? Do you want something more?" He wanted her to want his cock, but he knew she was shy. Or maybe it wasn't shyness. Maybe it was that she was uncertain as to what she actually enjoyed. He had a feeling she'd dated her fair share of losers in the past.

He reached with his free hand to get a condom and tore it open with his teeth. Her eyes widened as she saw what he was doing, but she didn't speak.

It wasn't normally his first position of the night, to take a woman from behind, but her backside was raised so perfectly, so temptingly, that he couldn't resist. He moved in behind her, nudging her legs just slightly apart, giving her time to object as he teased her with the tip of his erection. Her response was to lift her hips higher in a blatant invitation.

Oh, yeah. He was going in.

Hunter pushed his cock into Melanie with one thrust, dragging a groan from both of them. He was just savoring the sensation when he realized that she was nearly in the throes of an orgasm. Holy shit, that was hot.

He gripped her hips and slid a finger down and around to tease her clit.

The deep, throaty sob of satisfaction she gave was the best thing he'd heard in ages. "That's it, Melly. Come for me."

"I am," she said, and her pure wonderment made him swallow hard and start to move.

She felt incredible wrapped around him, and he lost himself in her, burying himself deep.

8

Melanie briefly considered the fact that she should be embarrassed for having an orgasm so quickly, but she was too busy having an orgasm to care. Damn, the man could do amazing things to her. It was something about his big hands, his hard, warm body, his teasing touch.

And his voice. It was deep, rumbling. Masculine. It didn't seem outrageous to do anything when he suggested it, when he coaxed her, encouraged.

She hadn't expected that he would just take her from behind. Then again, she hadn't expected he would massage her into such languid arousal. While still managing to kiss her. The very fact that it wasn't following the rehearsed choreography she was so accustomed to made it even sexier. Hunter seemed to do what occurred to him as each moment came, not because he had a sexual routine that he employed with all his lovers.

That was hot.

Which was why by the time he pushed inside her, she was beyond ready to come. He continued to thrust as the waves of ecstasy washed over her. Melanie gripped the bedsheet and allowed herself the freedom to call out his name. She couldn't believe that it was so easy to reach climax with him. She didn't consider herself a problem case, exactly, but it usually required a fair amount of effort. That Hunter brought her to the finish line in minutes astonished her and robbed her of any remaining rational thought.

His orgasm was less noisy than hers, but it satisfied her to hear him groan. "Holy shit," he said. "Melly, baby, that was unbelievable."

At first she hadn't been sure how she'd felt about him giving her a nickname that sprang from their porn-star joke, but now she found herself liking it. Melly was the kind of woman who had orgasms easily. She was calm, without constant to-do lists scrolling through her thoughts. To her surprise, she liked being Melly.

Hunter pulled back and flopped onto the bed next to her, face-first. She swallowed and rolled onto her side to face him, her lower back giving a twinge of protest at the angle she'd been in. Her lower back could suck it. That had been worth a little muscle pain. She blew her hair out of her eyes and gave him a smile. "Well. Hi."

"Hey." He stirred and gave her a smirk. "How was the massage?"

"Very satisfying."

Hunter propped himself up on one elbow, then reached out and smacked her on the ass. Melanie jumped from the slight sting, though it was more surprising than painful. "Ow! What was that for?"

"For being so damn desirable. I wanted to make that last a little longer, but you brought me to my knees."

Given the look on his face, she couldn't help but believe him. That in and of itself was enough to make her feel reassured. She had needed this, no question about it. "Thank you," she told him.

"Are you kidding me? I didn't hold a door open for you," he said, scoffing. "This was for both of us. No thanks need to be exchanged. That is what is weird. Not me touching your butt."

He had a point. It was an ingrained habit, one she clearly needed to break. "Maybe I should touch your butt and we'll be even."

"Be my guest."

Given that she'd been fantasizing about that ever since she'd seen him in his underwear, she was eager to go for it. Snuggling closer to him, she did a frontal spoon position.

"I like this already," he said, voice husky. "There are so many things I want to do to you. Good thing we have lots of time on our hands."

She slid her arm over his hip, feeling the heat of his skin, the tautness of his muscles. They could do this anytime they wanted for five more days, if you subtracted a day for the journey back to Chicago. Which of course she did, because that was the way her mind worked. That was never going to change. "Mmm. Sounds like a plan. Are you still going horseback riding with me tomorrow?"

"Of course."

She let her fingers wander over his butt and explore the firmness of his glutes. Wow. It felt as good as it looked.

"Does it stack up?" he asked. He was starting to sound sleepy.

"Very impressive."

She wondered if he would scoot away from her, making it clear this was just sex, nothing more. But he didn't. In fact, after pulling off the condom and depositing it on a tissue on the nightstand, he actually wrapped his arms around her and pulled her in closer.

"Think of this as a warm-up," he said. "An Intro to Orgasm course."

Melanie gave a soft laugh, feeling very relaxed and comfortable cocooned next to his warm body. "I wasn't a virgin, remember?"

"No, not technically. But before this trip is over I'm going to get you to really let go, Melly."

She thought she was doing pretty damn good so far. "I thought you were supposed to protect me from danger," she teased.

"How is great sex dangerous?"

Because when they got back to Chicago they wouldn't see each other again, and then he would be the gold standard by which she judged all future men. She didn't want to lose her head. Or worse, her heart.

"I'm not very athletic. I might pull something if I really let go." She'd go with flippant. He didn't need to know the direction her thoughts were taking.

"Always stretch first." He yawned.

If he knew she was being a little evasive, he didn't call her out on it. Though he probably didn't. Most men didn't think the way women did, hence the abundance of failed relationships. "Good plan."

"I can help you with the stretching if you'd like. Put your ankles on my shoulders and things like that."

Oh, Lord. "I'm good, thanks."

Hunter kissed her. "Then, quit complaining."

"I'm not complaining!" Was she? She didn't think she was. "But I'm going to go to sleep now. Good night."

"Good night, gorgeous."

Melanie shifted to roll onto her back.

"Stop wiggling."

"I was going to give you some room."

"I don't want room. I want you."

Melanie stilled. His eyes were closed, and he sounded only half-aware of what he was saying. He didn't mean anything by it. She knew that.

But for now she was just going to cuddle up against his warm body and enjoy being close to someone. Giving a sigh of relaxation, she closed her eyes and ended the first day of her vacation.

Never in a million years could she have predicted it would end this way, but she was proud of herself for going with the flow.

And she refused to wake up tomorrow with any regrets.

HUNTER HAD NEVER been into horseback riding. He didn't feel as though he could control the animal, and that pissed him off. So even though the horses used on the resort excursion were old and tame, he still felt as if he might fall off at any given moment. It didn't help his mood that Melanie looked completely comfortable and happy, trotting along the beach with her skin and eyes glowing.

He had woken up in the middle of the night sweating bullets, but he hadn't wanted to shift Melanie away from him, so he'd just dozed in and out of sleep. Then when he'd finally woken up, Melanie was already out of bed and in the shower. With the bathroom door locked. It wasn't how he had wanted to start the day. When she'd come back into the room she had cheerfully informed him he only had twenty minutes before departure, shattering his visual of Melanie climbing onto him and starting the morning out right with some lazy sex.

There had only been time for him to eat a muffin before he'd had to climb up on this beast. He was a man—he wanted breakfast, not baked goods. It was making him surly. As was the fact that he'd been wanting to explore Melanie from head to toe. She didn't look as if she was regretting the lack of morning sex. She looked happy, peaceful.

Which, now that he thought about it, was a good thing. She had needed to chill out a little. She deserved to be happy, and if riding a goddamn horse made her feel that way, then he'd deal. Maybe he could also flatter himself with the idea that she was feeling a little bit of afterglow.

Their guide was telling jokes and showing Melanie extra attention. Hunter found it incredibly irritating. Had she told him the porn-star story? He hoped not. It had been just a humorous inside joke between the two of them, and he had mentioned it himself to strangers, but now in hindsight that seemed like a bad idea. He didn't want her to receive inappropriate attention from guys on the resort because they thought she was a fun girl.

It was that concern that had him forcing his horse to walk a little faster so he could catch up with Melanie and her new boyfriend. He had to laugh at himself. He was jealous of the tour guide. It was ridiculous. Two days earlier he hadn't even known her, and now he was jealous. But while that was totally irrational, it wasn't out of line to be concerned about her safety if she was staying in character with the persona they had created.

So there.

Hunter came up so close and so quickly that the guide had to move his horse to the right to make room between himself and Melanie.

"Hey, amigo," the guide said with a big smile. "You're finally getting riding figured out, yes?"

"Yes."

Melanie gave him a look of contrition. "You're not having fun, are you? I'm sorry. I didn't know you don't like riding. I love it."

"I can tell. I'm fine. Don't worry about me." How long could this beach walk go? It couldn't be more than a couple of hours. "I'm getting to know my horse. We're buddies."

She laughed, and she sounded so carefree that he couldn't help but relax. The tour guide fell back to talk to another couple, and Hunter took the moment of privacy to warn her. "Hey, uh, I know I started the whole Melly Ambrosia thing, but I don't think you should tell people you're in the film industry. I don't want guys getting creepy on you. It might bring you some unwanted attention."

She gave him a look of disapproval. "You're right, you did start it. But for your information, I didn't tell him anything of the sort. One, he knows my name because it was on the excursion package. Two, I'm not dumb. And three, he assumed you're my boyfriend. He's just being friendly, not gross. It's his job. I'm sure he wants a tip at the end of the tour."

"If people are assuming you're my girlfriend, then you should act like it." Wow. That sounded super assholish. He meant it to be flirtatious, not possessive.

Her eyes widened, and she leaned forward slightly,

petting her horse as if it reassured her. The breeze tossed her hair into her face. "What is that supposed to mean?"

"Nothing. Never mind." There was really no way to explain his feelings. At least none that he was comfortable with. Hell, he didn't even know what his feelings were.

"We're just…fooling around, right?" she asked, suddenly sounding uncertain.

Great. She thought he was angling for some sort of relationship. It was usually the other way around—the guy was supposed to worry that the woman was assuming too much. The fact that she was thinking he was having ooey-gooey thoughts after a brief but intense sexual encounter was downright humiliating. So he liked her. Big deal.

"Yes. We're just fooling around. While we're here in Mexico."

"It's a vacation fling?"

Her expression was inscrutable.

"Yes."

"So we don't need to talk about what happens when we get back to Chicago because nothing will happen. Correct?"

This was a minefield. He was certain of it. She was setting a trap for him. If she thought he was going to avoid it by disagreeing, therefore condemning himself to awkward expectations, then she took him for a fool. He wasn't stupid. He was not the guy for Melanie. She needed Mr. Touchy Feely, not Stonewall Jackson. When they got back home they would go their separate ways. He would hole up in his stark apartment and work and exercise, and she would meet a nice guy who golfed and would go antiques shopping with her. This was just one of those things they had fallen into and while it was mutually pleasurable, it couldn't go anywhere.

"Correct."

"Thanks for making that clear."

She was annoyed, though he couldn't pinpoint exactly why, whether it was because she wanted there to be something more or because she didn't like that he was just putting it out there. "You're welcome."

But that was the wrong answer, because Melanie rolled her eyes and kicked the flank of her horse, setting off into a trot and leaving him in her sandy wake. His own horse whinnied and reared his head. "Don't worry, buddy," he told him. "We're not going to chase her. She just wants to be left alone."

This day certainly wasn't playing out the way he had intended. Not even freaking close.

9

DIDN'T MEN KNOW that when you walked off in a huff, or in her case, galloped off on a horse, you wanted them to follow? Melanie had made it clear that she was annoyed and in her mind, Hunter's role was to catch up and coax a confession out of her so they could work things through. The fact that he was too obtuse to realize it incensed her even more. So she rode on and occasionally glanced back, wondering how he had managed to sour her mood so completely in the course of ten minutes.

She wasn't a moron. She knew this was a vacation fling. But the fact that he had to point it out—as if he was terrified she might get ideas and fall in love with him—was beyond frustrating. The sheer arrogance of men astounded her. Why couldn't she have some of that moxie? To go through life confident in her assumptions that men would want her would be extremely liberating.

Well, she would show Hunter exactly how she felt. She was not ready for a relationship in any way, shape or form. She was barely twenty-four hours out of the last one, and look at how unsatisfying it had been. She needed a breather and to assess what she really wanted, what she was looking for in a partner. The fact that Hunter assumed that because she had ovaries she would be clamoring to lock and load a man into a relationship was sexist and frustrating. She could do casual sex. Actually, she was going to *put* the casual into sex, thank you very much.

Hadn't she proved that last night? Jeez. It was safe to say that she had not been thinking about her future or how to hook Hunter permanently when she'd slipped into bed wearing only her panties.

Now he was simultaneously worried that other men on the resort might find her attractive if she maintained the Melly persona, and concerned that if he appeared to be her boyfriend she might get some crazy idea in her head that he was her boyfriend. Apparently, she was supposed to walk some magical mystery line where she was friendly but not too friendly with him or anyone else who had a penis. Really. Where did men come up with this garbage?

Determined to shake it off, she rode ahead of the tour group, then doubled back. She had ridden a lot as a child, but almost never had the money to do it now. It was an expensive hobby. It felt great to be back in the saddle, and she couldn't help but calm down in response to the sweet, gentle eyes of her ancient horse, Ariel. By the time she fell in line beside Hunter again, she was composed and determined to make him so hot for her he wouldn't be able to maintain his seat.

"Having fun?" he asked her.

"Always," she said breezily. "Isn't that the point of vacation?"

He nodded, looking cautious.

"To lie in the sun, explore a little, mindlessly grope

a stranger into the wee hours of the night." That didn't come out right. She was trying to be sexy, and she just sounded bitchy. They needed a do-over today. Two hours in, and they were off the rails.

"Is that what we were doing? Mindlessly groping?" He sounded offended.

"I believe that goes along with casual vacation sex, yes." Not that she'd ever done it before, but it seemed to be part of the commonly accepted definition.

"That makes it sound so impersonal. It's not like that. We're becoming friends. We like each other."

Melanie decided to give up. She had no clue what was going on inside that man's head, and the truth was, she was starting to think she didn't want to. It was probably a dark cave of fear of commitment and double standards.

"Okay," she told him simply.

"What, we're not friends?"

Oh, yeah, he was offended. He looked downright curdled. Of course, he'd been looking disagreeable since she'd gotten out of the shower and reminded him of their excursion. "Of course we're friends." Though it wasn't as if they particularly knew each other. She was familiar with his expressions, his scent, and had gotten a very brief and abridged description of his childhood. That was about it. But this wasn't how she wanted to behave. It wasn't how she wanted to feel.

She was projecting onto Hunter. He hadn't done a damn thing wrong. This was about Ian, and she swallowed hard, ashamed that she had let herself make conclusions about Hunter's thoughts, motives, actions. If she wanted to know what he was thinking, for pity's sake, she just needed to open her trap and ask the man.

"I'm sorry, Hunter. I didn't mean to sound so weird. I actually really appreciate you being honest with me. I like that we're both clear on the fact that we're intending to enjoy our time here and enjoy each other."

He eyed her carefully. "Did I push too much yesterday? I'm sorry if I did. I wasn't trying to be an opportunist."

"I'm the one who jumped into bed naked. No, you didn't push."

"I don't want you to regret this. I want you to have fun, not wonder what I'm thinking or feeling."

"What are you feeling?" Damn it, why did she go there? She was annoyed with herself for being so wishy-washy and back and forth.

"I'm feeling damn lucky, that's how I'm feeling. I never expected a week like this. Or a woman like you."

In the pursuit of being open and honest, she said, "I feel as though I should mention that I've never done this—had a vacation affair. I don't exactly know what I'm doing, so be patient with me. I get that the general concept is we don't see each other once we get back to Chicago."

"That is the general concept. We need to agree that we'll stick to the vacation fling parameters. Shake on it?" Hunter stuck his hand out to her.

She felt as though she was agreeing to buy a car. "Can we pinky swear instead? Shaking hands makes it feel like a business arrangement."

Hunter laughed. "Yes, we can pinky swear." He hooked hers with his and gave her a smile. "I pinky swear that I'm going to make you so hot later tonight you won't even remember you're from Chicago."

Yes, please. She felt her nipples tighten. "I'm not. I'm from Kentucky."

"You're killing me." He tried to lean closer to her, but his horse skittered in the opposite direction. "By the way, I want you to tell people we're together," he said, looking very determined. "I screwed up big-time making a joke out of the film-star thing. I never should have exposed you like that."

"I think I exposed myself," she said, going for a joke. "But just to you."

He did laugh with her, but he also added, "I'm serious, Melanie. I want you to make it clear to people we're together. I don't want anyone crossing any lines, and I definitely don't want you wandering around the resort by yourself."

It wasn't as if she'd been clamoring to get away from him. She had no idea why he was suddenly so worked up. But she could pretend to be his girlfriend. On one condition. "Fine. But you have to talk to me, open up. If I'm going to pretend to be your girlfriend, I have to know details about you."

He made a face, but he nodded. "Probably not necessary, but if that's what you want."

"It is." If she was going to be snuggled up against him at night, and holding hands around the resort during the day, she wanted to know his middle name and where he'd grown up. Why he'd joined the marines. What he wanted for his future. All of it. "It will be fun, Hunter. You can get to know me, too."

The look he gave her was so scorching and sexy that she actually wobbled a little in the saddle. "I intend to."

Wow. Melanie decided she was done with this whole group-tour thing. They were walking back into the barn area, and she was grateful. She wanted some private time with Hunter. He dismounted first, and when it was her turn he reached up to help her down.

Normally, she could dismount on her own with no assistance, but she was so rattled by sudden arousal and the memory of Hunter thrusting inside her that she fell out of the saddle harder than she intended. She saw the momentary wince on his face when he caught her, and she remembered he had an injury.

"Oh, my God, your arm," she said, instantly fretting. She landed on the sand and stepped away from him, feeling horrible. "Are you okay?"

"I'm fine." His voice was rough, his lips pursed.

He wasn't fine. But her Hunter 101 class had taught her to leave it alone. He would not appreciate her fawning over him or repeatedly offering him sympathy. He was a Tough Guy.

So instead of fussing over him, she just put her arms around his neck and gave him a soft kiss on the lips. He stiffened even further.

"What was that for?" he asked.

Giving him a smile, she shrugged. "For the crowd? Or just because I felt like it? Maybe both."

When she dropped her arms, she slipped her hand into his, knowing that despite his demand they act like a couple, it would make him uncomfortable. She laid her head on his shoulder. "Can I call you pookie?"

"Look who found her inner smart-ass."

"Who?" She pretended to search the beach.

Hunter gave her such a long look she burst out laughing.

An older woman patted Melanie on the arm as she walked past. "You two lovebirds are so cute together."

The woman was clearly drunk, because Hunter looked anything but cute—more as if he had indigestion. "Thank you," she said anyway.

"Is this your honeymoon?"

"No, we've been married for five years. That's why he looks so grumpy."

Hunter snorted.

"Well, maybe it's time to have a baby, then," the woman said in a singsong voice.

Definitely drunk.

"Not this week," Hunter said.

Melanie was amused. She waved to the woman and tugged on Hunter's hand, pulling him away with her. When they were out of earshot, she said, "So do you want kids someday?"

"Sure. Why? Most people do."

"Don't get defensive. Jeez. I was just curious." Hunter was a tender guy, despite the fact that he liked to think he wasn't. She would bet money he'd melt like butter in the microwave over a baby.

"Do you?" he asked.

"Someday." Melanie didn't have the urgent desire at the moment, but she definitely enjoyed children. "I think that woman was plastered."

"She did smell like rum," he conceded.

"It's only eleven in the morning."

"She's on vacation. Don't judge. And just for the record, I think talking about whether or not we want kids falls outside the scope of vacation sex."

He was right. But she didn't mean anything by it. She was just making conversation. Melanie smacked his arm. "Hey. I pinky swore we're just having fun, and we are. So why can't I talk about whatever pops into my head?"

"I guess there's no reason you can't."

"What's your drink of choice? Just beer?"

"Yeah. I'm not a big drinker. You can't drink out on the base in Afghanistan so I got used to doing without. Then I got stateside and got wasted on just a couple of drinks. It wasn't worth it. I'm sticking to beer. What about you?"

"I'm a wine girl."

"A wino?" He smirked.

"Now who's the smart-ass?"

Hunter changed the subject. "Can we get some breakfast? I'm starving. Pastries in the morning are for kids and French people. I need some eggs and bacon."

"Every day is going to be about your stomach, isn't it?" They were walking back toward the main building of the resort. He was still holding her hand, which surprised her. Sure, he wanted everyone to think they were together, but she had him pegged for a no-public-displays-of-affection kind of guy. Although he had definitely been all about the postsex snuggle the night before.

She was doing it again. Projecting. Ugh.

He shot her a wicked grin. "That's not the only physical need that requires frequent satisfaction."

Perfect. He had a gift for making her instantly aroused. How did he do that? It was some kind of sexual voodoo. "How frequent?"

"Morning, noon and night."

Whatever. He was clearly in the mood to tease her. "Don't exaggerate. I was asking a serious question."

"I'm being totally serious. That's my ideal."

"Three times a day? That's not even possible!" She didn't think. Was it?

He gave her a long look. "Of course it's possible. There isn't a grace period after sex."

"But…who has time for that?"

"I said *ideal*. Under circumstances where there's nothing else you have to do—like being on vacation." His thumb rubbed across the palm of her hand. "So why not?"

Why not, indeed? "Umm…" Lordy, she felt both scandalized and quite intrigued. The man was ambitious.

"I had high hopes for waking up in the best way possible this morning, as a matter of fact, but you snuck off into the shower. Tomorrow I'm going to have to get the jump on you." He winked.

So that explained their earlier tension. He'd been wanting breakfast meat and her, and she'd been all about getting out the door and onto a horse. "Oh. I didn't realize that. You didn't say anything."

"You were so cheerful and efficient. I didn't think you could be talked into ditching your excursion."

That made her seem so predictable. "You'll never know unless you try," she countered.

"Oh, yeah?"

"Yeah." She was really getting into the idea. "We could go back to the room right now and see what happens when you do try."

"I need breakfast first."

Of course he did. She was trying to be spontaneous and sexy, and he wanted bacon. She couldn't help but be amused. "Of course."

"But then you should be prepared to be swept off

your feet. You don't have anything planned for this afternoon, do you?"

"I was hoping to go back to the pool," she answered.

"The pool will still be there tomorrow. Today we're locking the door and making the people in the next room jealous."

That sounded promising. "Then let's feed you some protein and put out the do-not-disturb sign."

HUNTER GRINNED AT MELANIE. She sounded intrigued by the concept of spending the afternoon in bed. He couldn't believe she'd never done it before. It seemed unfathomable for someone her age—not that he knew what that was, exactly. "How old are you anyway?"

She glanced back at him as he opened the restaurant door for her. "Twenty-eight. Why?"

"I don't know. Just curious." Then, because it seemed like he should share, he added, "I'm thirty."

"And you don't look a day over twenty-nine and a half."

She really had found her inner smart-ass. He chuckled. "Thanks. You look ageless, timeless, priceless."

"Oh, God." Melanie burst out laughing. "That debonair act does not work for you. Just…no."

"What? You don't think I'm suave?" Hell, he knew he wasn't. But it was funny that she already had him pegged. He was honest, sometimes too honest, and didn't know how to give seductive and charming speeches. But he could promise to give her lots of pleasure.

"You look great in a suit, but you are no James Bond. For which I'm grateful. Because then I would most likely die at the hands of a villain after sleeping with you. That seems to be the fate of all his beautiful ladies."

"Half of them are spies and he knows it, but he nails them anyway. I couldn't do that." He pulled Melanie's chair out for her and when she sat down, he bent and kissed the back of her neck, shifting her hair for access. "Darling."

She shivered then giggled. "Okay, maybe you've got a little James Bond in you."

He sat down across from her, pleased with her reaction. "Thanks."

"So you wouldn't sleep with me if you knew I was sending secrets to the enemy?"

"Nope. I'm a patriot. I wasn't on active duty for the paycheck." He set his sunglasses down on the table. "Can I go get my eggs now?" Not to fixate on his breakfast, but damn, he was hungry.

"Yes, please. Feed yourself before you expire from malnourishment."

The words were teasing. Her smile was sweet, tender. As if she liked him. Cared about him. Warning bells clanged in Hunter's head, but he chose to ignore them. They were both very clear on this being just a fun few days together. He didn't need to worry that Melanie was getting attached to him, who didn't deserve her attachment. There was no reason he couldn't enjoy her company and her casual affection, right?

"Thank you." He stood up and proceeded to the around-the-world-themed buffet to make himself the biggest plate of food he could manage. It looked like a landfill heap by the time he was finished loading up: crepes, a breakfast burrito, kippers and potato pancakes. It was like a victory for his stomach right there on a porcelain plate.

Melanie drank a cup of coffee and nibbled on some melon chunks, and he shook his head in disbelief as he watched her. Life would be a hell of a lot easier if he could sustain himself on melon chunks, but that wasn't happening anytime soon.

When he was finished he felt a thousand times better, and guilty for being such a crabass that morning. As they left the restaurant he suggested they poke their heads into some of the gift shops along the way. One had cigars, another jewelry and a third offered bottles of wine. "Let's get some champagne," he said. "To celebrate."

"Celebrate what?" she asked, even though she looked pleased at the idea.

"Freedom from snow and icy wind that freezes your extremities in thirty seconds." He picked out a bottle. "This good?"

"Sure."

She stood very close to him while he paid, the kind of close that bespoke intimacy. He liked it, he had to admit. This was what he had been missing when he was deployed. Companionship. The right to touch someone easily, familiarly. Catching her off guard, he kissed the side of her head.

This was dicey territory. Here they had just agreed there was nothing more to it than sex, and yet they both seemed intent on meandering into intimacy.

"Is it your anniversary?" the perky young clerk asked.

"Yes," he lied, for no particular reason whatsoever. He just kind of wanted it to be a special day. Not just another day to trudge through, but a "carpe diem, he was on vacation with a hot woman" kind of day. That wasn't breaking their bargain; it was just enjoying the time together while he could. She wanted to talk. He wanted to cuddle. No harm in that.

Being single was not what he had expected for this phase of his life. He'd accidentally done things in reverse. He'd been with Danielle while he was halfway around the world, and now that he was back and really wanted the companionship, he was alone. Not what he'd had in mind. But he knew he was right in his conviction to fly solo for a while. There was a reason his relationships kept going south, and as far as he could tell, the common denominator was him. He had to figure out what that was about before he attempted anything lasting again.

Melanie made a sound in the back of her throat at his outright lie, but she didn't protest.

"That's great," the clerk enthused, bagging their purchase and handing it back. "Congratulations. How many years?"

"Five," Hunter said, echoing Melanie's earlier claim as he accepted the bottle. "Thanks. We're heading back to the room."

She winked at Melanie. "Lucky girl."

Melanie laughed.

When they left, she said, "You're very bad, Hunter."

"You started the whole anniversary thing." He eyed the cigar shop. "Can I get one? Do you mind?"

"No, not at all. I'm going to get myself a dolphin necklace to remind me of this trip."

He swatted her butt as she went into the jewelry

shop. "I'll give you something to remember, sweetheart."

She rolled her eyes at him, but she also smiled, which made him smile in return. They were just a couple of grinning fools. Feeling like an idiot, Hunter went into the cigar shop and tried to focus on making a selection. He could kick himself for suggesting shopping when they could already be back at the room, but he knew it was important to get a grip on his libido and let Melanie set the pace.

After five minutes of chatting with the store clerk and going into the humidor, Hunter felt more confident that he could maintain his emotional distance from Melanie for five more days and just enjoy himself. No confusing the damn issue. They weren't celebrating an anniversary. They weren't a couple. Playing house with each other revealed a little too much about what they both wanted, but—for both of their sakes—he was determined to avoid.

After purchasing a cigar, he wandered over to the jewelry shop to see how Melanie was faring with her souvenir. She had approximately seventeen necklaces laid out on the counter in front of her.

"Which one?" she asked him, waving her hand over the whole lot.

There was a lot of dolphin action happening on that countertop. "Uh…I don't know." They all looked the same. A leaping dolphin on a chain. But he also knew Melanie was the kind of woman who liked to be methodical and ask a lot of questions, so he feared they could be there for another hour if he didn't give an opinion. "This one?" He pointed to one that looked more playful than the others.

She frowned. "You don't think this one is too big?"

"Yes, it is, actually." He was already learning—Melanie's pointless question meant that that option was not going to make her happy. "I like this one." He chose one at random and gave it to the clerk. "Can you box this up for us?"

Melanie stiffened and made a squawk of protest. "But I'm not sure if that's the one I want."

"She who hesitates ends up with no dolphin necklace. Or one she will never really be sure about. Just pick one and embrace it. You're not buying a house, babe."

He was probably being a little heavy-handed, but it was something he'd noticed about her: she pondered and pondered and then was never really satisfied with the result.

"But..."

Hunter pulled out his wallet and gave his credit card to the clerk. He hoped like hell that necklace wasn't two thousand dollars or something insane.

"You don't have to pay for it," she protested.

"I want to." He saw with relief as the total came up on the register that it was only twenty-five bucks. He could swing that, though he would have been willing to go into debt if it made Melanie relax and let loose.

He leaned over and kissed her on the head in a move that contradicted everything he had just told himself. Wow. He was not keeping it in the casual-sex zone. He absently thanked the shopkeeper as she handed him the purchase. This wasn't good. Not good at all.

But Melanie smiled up at him, making his gesture feel worth the risk. "Well, if you insist." Then she stunned him by leaning over and kissing him softly on the lips in full view of the clerk. "You ready?"

Ready to hunker down and keep his head out of his ass. Ready to make sure his emotional walls were firmly in place. Ready to focus solely on making Melanie scream in bed. "Hell, yeah."

10

MELANIE WAS GLAD the day had turned around after starting out so badly. She didn't know how to conduct herself after sleeping with a man she'd known only sixteen hours. She had been uncertain of what Hunter was thinking, afraid that being impulsive—as great as it had been—was a poor choice.

It had felt fantastic to end the day from hell on such a high note, and she didn't want it to be messy or complicated. They had pinky sworn it was nothing but sex, and that was liberating.

Hunter was right—she did need to stop thinking so much. It stole a lot of the enjoyment from making a final choice. Whether it was a dolphin necklace, a risotto or a man, she invariably wound up questioning whether she had made the right pick, since she had debated it so endlessly. This really could be the most freeing vacation she'd ever had. She had intended it to be a sex fest with Ian, but it was turning out to be about more than that. It was about learning to embrace life and not worry so much. Along with being a sex fest.

Which was why she was going to go back to the room with Hunter and enjoy him without thinking it meant a single thing. On the path back to their part of the hotel, Hunter paused, setting the bottle of champagne down on the ground. "What are you doing?" she asked.

He fished her necklace out of the bag and pulled off the tag. "I thought you might want to wear this." Undoing the clasp, he came around behind her and dropped it down over her face onto her chest.

"Oh, thanks." She shivered a little at the feel of his warm fingers on her neck as he hooked the clasp.

He lifted her hair up and over it, pausing to kiss the tender spot below her ear. "You're welcome."

Her hair dropped back down, and he moved away. Melanie had never stopped to think that maybe what she had been craving from Ian wasn't a sex fest—it was this. Touch. It was a natural craving to feel someone's fingers brush your skin, slide through your hair. As a little girl, she had loved to have her hair braided, to roll herself in a blanket with her cousins, to climb on her mother's lap. It wasn't as easy to achieve that type of physical closeness as an adult, and she had been searching for it. Ironically, taking her clothes off for Ian had not fulfilled that need.

Yet a simple gesture from Hunter had.

Oh, yeah. She had a lot to learn about herself and what she wanted. But right now all she knew was that she wanted Hunter. For the next four days he was hers. This was uncharted territory for her—being with someone without expectation—but she liked the freedom.

"How long did you and Danielle date?" she asked. Because that was a smart topic to bring up en route to a nooner.

He glanced over at her. His expression was inscrutable. "Eighteen months. Why?"

"Just curious." She was so bad at this casual sex thing. Then again, she wasn't that great at relationships, either. The whole male-female thing seemed to befuddle her.

She fingered the necklace dangling down almost to her breasts and reminded herself it was about learning not to control the situation. To just enjoy it.

When they reached their room, Hunter suggested they sit on the veranda and watch the dolphins. He pulled out two glasses from the bar area, popped the cork on the champagne and poured. She went out onto the patio and sank down into a chair with a relaxed sigh, accepting the glass of bubbly he handed her.

"A toast," he said, raising his glass in the direction of hers.

She thought he was going to say something about sun, surf, champagne.

Nope. Not even close.

"To Ian, for being the dumbest piece of shit I've ever met. I owe him big-time."

Really? What happened to channeling James Bond? That had been sexier. Yet she had to laugh. Hunter always managed to amuse her. "I'm not drinking to Ian."

"Why not? If it wasn't for him we wouldn't be here right now."

"I don't think him dumping me merits raising a glass in his honor." She clinked her glass against his. "To fun. How's that?"

He raised his eyebrows but didn't say a word. He tapped her glass back and lifted his own to his lips. Melanie took a sip, watching the dolphins. They looked as if they were perpetually smiling, but she wondered whether the animals enjoyed each other's company or if it was more like how she felt about her fellow humans on the L. Irritated at the constant sharing of space.

But then one dolphin got on the other's back. "Oh!" she said, a little startled. She felt more than a little awkward watching the situation playing out mere feet from her.

Hunter laughed. "I guess we can't suggest they get a room."

"Should we go back inside? They might want to be alone." Despite her words she found herself unable to glance away, which made it even more embarrassing.

"I'm not sure they particularly care about privacy, but I would definitely like some with you." Hunter stood up and reached his hand out to help her up.

Melanie took his hand, and wondered if she was blushing. She certainly felt overheated. It felt so different to be anticipating going to bed with him than with any of the boyfriends she'd had. The comfort level was missing, yet the sheer depth of the attraction she felt for him made her skin tingle, her heart race, her chest heave with quick, anxious breaths. It felt as if the night before had been a quick and unexpected preview. She had a feeling this would be more exploratory, and that made her both excited and nervous.

Part of her wanted to jump on Hunter, take him straight to the bed and get it going on, but at the same time she wanted to push herself, and see if she could allow him to lead her through a truly sensual experience. This wasn't about a to-do list, efficiency. It was about sensuality.

She was still holding her glass in her hand, and as they went back inside she drained the last bit of her champagne. Hunter took the flute from her and set it along with his on the TV stand. There was a pause while he looked at her with a mischievous and sexy smile. Then he reached out and cupped her cheek with his hand.

"You're very beautiful," he said. "Like I said, I'm a lucky man."

As if. She was feeling like the one who had scored here. This could have been the most miserable week of her life and yet here she was. Enjoying herself, and then some. "Thank you for saving my vacation," she murmured.

"My pleasure." Hunter closed the gap between them and kissed her.

It was more tender than she was expecting, and it caught her off guard. Her shoulders relaxed, her lips parted on a sigh and she felt a flutter deep inside her core. It felt natural to reach up, snake her arms around him and caress the back of his neck. The kiss turned into many, their mouths meeting and parting only to be drawn together again by a mutual desire. It went on and on, and Hunter made no move to take her to the bed. His hand had dropped to her arm, and he stroked her with a soft, feathery touch.

She felt as if she already knew his mouth, his scent, his height. When he shifted her closer to him, it felt easy, her anxiety gone. There was no hurry, and with each simple kiss, her arousal smoldered like forgotten embers. It had been forever since she'd experienced such a fully clothed make-out session. Eventually, his hand slid all the way down her arm, and he laced his fingers with hers, lifting her arm up and out. He kissed a path from her wrist to her elbow and on up past her shoulder, burying his mouth into her neck. Shivering, she tipped her head back to give him greater access.

And he claimed he wasn't charming. This was pretty damn charming in her book.

If there had been music they would have been dancing. As if it were a tango, Melanie lifted her leg, wanting to wrap herself into him and have her body touching his everywhere possible. He gave a low murmur of approval in the back of his throat, then startled her by scooping her up in his arms and walking her to the bed.

Oh, wow. She had never experienced that before. He lifted her as if she was nothing, and while her first instinct was to protest and mention his injury, she clamped her lips shut and vowed not to destroy the moment. Just feel it. He deposited her down on the mattress and smoothed her hair off her face. Then he kissed her again and guided her leg back up to where it had been when they were standing. Only now he was wedged between her legs, and she could revel in being surrounded by his arms, and feel his erection press against her hip.

He pulled back and teased his fingers down over her chest, not lingering on her breasts, just brushing them, before doing the same to her midsection and her inner thighs. It was light and worshipful and driving her completely and utterly insane. If he wanted her to squirm, this was a surefire way to achieve it. Slowly, carefully, he undid the buttons on her shirt one at a time, taking long seconds to kiss each new expanse of skin that was exposed by his efforts. His tongue slipped over the swell of first one breast, then the other, but didn't shift her bra out of the way.

Hunter continued on down until her entire shirt was open and his tongue was teasing into her belly button. She squirmed, especially when he made a slick trail down to the waistband of her shorts and popped the snap with his teeth. "Oh, Hunter," she moaned, for no particular reason other than wanting him to understand exactly what he was doing to her.

But he paused, lifting his head from her navel. "Yes?"

"Nothing."

"Okay," he said, sounding lazy and relaxed.

With devastating casualness, he took her zipper down so slowly she wanted to shove his hand out of the way and do it herself. It was sweet torture. When her shorts fell open, he nuzzled down into the revealed space, rubbing his lips over her sex. With only her panties between the heat of his touch and her clitoris, she hissed, the ache deep inside her damn near painful.

"You're enjoying teasing me, aren't you?" she asked him.

"Yep. But I'm teasing myself, too, you know."

"You can be masochistic on your own time." She wiggled her hips to encourage greater interaction.

"We have five days. I'm not looking to rush anything." But he took hold of her waistband and eased her shorts down with a slow pace that had her closing her eyes, her nipples peaking.

Then he kissed her mound, her panties dampening through from both his tongue and from her own desire. She felt hot, moist, aroused everywhere, and when he peeled her panties down slowly, she grabbed his head, needing something to hold on to. He left them barely past her hips, which didn't allow her the freedom she wanted, the ability to spread her legs and have him move his hands or mouth over her. She was about to complain, vigorously, but then he lightly scratched over the front of her with his fingers, while his mouth sucked on her hip bone. It was an unfamiliar sensation, giving the impression that he was drawing her out of herself, and she raised her hips instinctively.

"I love the way you taste," he murmured against her skin. "The way you feel, the way you smell. Like sun and sex."

Oh, my. She was pretty sure no one had ever said anything like that to her. It was the strangest and sexiest compliment she'd ever received.

Hunter shifted farther upward, giving her a brief but deep kiss before undoing her bra under her back and dragging the straps down her arms with his teeth. He made a sensual project out of the process, lingering at points along the way to lick and kiss her in places she wouldn't have thought would be pleasing, like the inside of her elbows and the soft translucent skin on the back of her wrist. Even her palm felt erogenous when his tongue flickered over it. By the time he returned to her now-bare breasts to take a nipple into his mouth, she was shifting her head left and right and digging her heels into the mattress.

But still he didn't hurry. He cupped the fullness of her breasts, teased and laved at her nipples with his tongue, sucked the swell of her breasts, his finger slipping inside her panties to stroke her moist heat. It was a rhythmic touch, but not a deep one, and it only added to her pleasure and frustration. He raised his slumberous eyes to stare at her intently, his nostrils flaring. He sat back on his haunches and yanked his shirt off over his head. She would never get tired of ogling his chest, and she reached out and fanned her hand over his warm skin. With the pad of her thumb, she teased his nipple.

Then she had an idea. A way to return the torture.

Melanie sat up and reached for the button on his shorts.

"Hey," he said, when she popped them open. "Who said you could do that?"

"I don't need to ask permission," she replied, giving him a saucy smile. She nudged her shorts down farther and got up on her knees. "Now it's my turn to taste."

She pulled his zipper down and had the satisfaction of hearing him suck in a breath when she lifted his cock out of his boxers and into her hand. His palms landed on her shoulders.

"What are you doing, Melly?"

The nickname really was growing on her. "What's it look like I'm doing?" Or more accurately, what did it feel like?

She closed her mouth over him.

He groaned. His fingers tightened on her shoulders. "You don't have to do this."

There was no point in wasting her breath telling him she wanted to. She would just show him. Using her hand to lead the way for her mouth, she went up and down on his shaft, pausing to twirl her tongue over the tip. When her rhythm was steady and sure, based on indicators from him as to what pace he liked the best, she reached out and held on to his hip, releasing his erection and using only her mouth.

Then she did her banana trick.

"Holy shit," Hunter said, jerking back.

But whereas he would have pulled out of her mouth

entirely, she held on to him, taking him deep a second time. The ultimate moment of triumph came when he started to piston his hips, taking over with a rough groan. He thrust in and out for a minute before yanking himself completely out of her mouth. This time she let him. When she looked up at him, wiping her damp and swollen lips, he was shaking his head.

"You're dangerous," he told her.

She thought it was the best compliment she'd ever gotten. She smiled up at him. "I'm not sorry."

"Neither am I." Then he leaned forward and gave her shoulders a shove.

"Ah!" She wobbled precariously, then gave up and fell backward onto the bed with a bounce.

Not a position she liked to be in, but he moved over her so quickly she didn't have time to be embarrassed or protest or artfully arrange herself. Hunter jerked her shorts and panties off from where they were still caught on her ankles and tossed them onto the tile floor. She expected him to move over her and enter her, but that was not what he did. He dropped down and drove into her with his tongue.

Given how ready she already was, his action nearly had her bolting off the bed.

"Oh, my," she cried out, wanting to add a nasty swearword but stopping herself at the last minute.

"Open your legs wider," he urged.

Not a problem. She could do that.

After she obeyed, he paused again in working her over to say, "Yell for me, Melly. Scream my name. So loud the neighbors hear."

What? She couldn't do that. There was no way she could do that. Could she?

When he hooked his finger inside her as his tongue slid over her clitoris, she realized that, yes, she could in fact scream loud enough to disturb the neighbors. Her orgasm swept over her with such intensity she almost knocked him off her. But Hunter held on to her thighs, hard, and didn't let her break his rhythm. At that moment she cared about nothing but the way Hunter made her feel.

As the throes of ecstasy settled down into shuddery aftershocks, she swallowed hard, moistening her lips with her tongue. "Oh, Hunter."

"Oh, Melly," he said with a victorious grin. "Now, that was hot." He had moved over her and gave her a quick kiss before positioning himself between her thighs.

She didn't know if she could take any more stimulation, but then he teased his erection over her, and she was suddenly sure she could take a whole lot more. "Hunter," she urged, when it was clear he wasn't going to do anything other than torture.

"Melanie," he said, mocking her whiny voice in a lighthearted tease.

Okay, his self-restraint might be admirable in other circumstances, but at the moment it was just frustrating. So if he was going to tease, she could do it right back. With a grin, she clamped her legs shut, forcing him back a little.

His head tilted as he realized what she had just done. "Oh, someone is looking for trouble."

Melanie reached out and stroked his penis. "Did I find it?" she asked, feeling flirty and sassy.

"Definitely." He gripped her knee and paused, as if

he was gauging her response to an aggressive move. "Let me show you how much fun trouble can be."

"Please do." It was the first time in the history of her sexuality that she had effectively turned the tables on a man without him realizing it. She was getting exactly what she wanted.

He understood that she was giving him permission to shove her leg to the side, and that was exactly what he did. He sheathed himself with a condom, and then he was inside her. Hunter had a determined look of concentration on his face that she found absolutely charming and sexy all at once. He was Bond again, all studied and carefully calculated moves. She wanted to see him lose control the way she had, but it wasn't going to happen now, that was clear to her. He was enjoying himself, but keeping the lid on tightly.

She was willing to accept that since it felt so damn good. He had serious skill, and the intensity of his focus on her made her feel like the hottest thing since a Southern summer. When he gritted his teeth and exploded, she gripped his back and watched in total satisfaction. With a groan he collapsed on the bed, pulling her onto him.

"Damn, you are sexy as hell," he said.

"You're not so bad yourself." Very possibly the best she'd ever had, but she didn't want his head to swell. Well. Not for another ten minutes, at least.

Outside the room they heard a giant splash from the dolphin grotto.

"Victory all around," Hunter said. "That dolphin and I both managed to score. I feel proud."

Melanie laughed. "Forced confinement does funny things to a girl."

"Great. That's really ego boosting."

That made her laugh even harder. "I meant let down our guard, not be talked into something we don't want to do."

"Just stop talking before I cry."

That was the most ridiculous thing she'd ever heard. She was giggling so hard she was vibrating both of their bodies. "Can't. Breathe."

Hunter flipped her on her back so suddenly and unexpectedly that the air was robbed from her lungs. Not only did she stop laughing, she felt desire spark all over again at the determined look on his face.

"Don't talk. Just feel," he told her, before he descended down on her again with his tongue.

She definitely had no words. Only moans of pleasure.

11

Hunter was in a whole hell of a lot better mood for their zip line excursion than he had been for the horseback riding the day before. Not only had he enjoyed a lengthy sex session with Melanie the night before, he'd woken up with an erection, and this time she had indulged him in getting rid of it. Not that he thought it was a particular hardship for her. Melanie was definitely loosening up. It was damn hot to watch her letting go, and he was enjoying himself more than he had in a long-ass time.

They were at the adventure park with a bunch of other tourists, listening to the instructions of the staff. Two guys who gave their names as Celso and Gil were entertaining everyone with their humorous safety spiel, but Hunter was only half listening. He kept stealing glances at Melanie sitting next to him. The harness they had clipped her into outlined some of his favorite spots on her body. Her thighs were crisscrossed by the straps, which repeatedly drew his attention to the apex of her legs, and when she shifted slightly in front of him, he could see that the straps also served to push her butt up in a perky manner that was driving him nuts. He would have thought he'd be sexually satisfied at least for a few hours, but it seemed that the more of Melanie he had, the more he wanted.

But when she glanced over at him, he forgot about his lust. She was chewing on her bottom lip. Hunter already recognized that as a sign that she was nervous and worried. "What's wrong?"

"I don't know if I can do this. It looks so…free falling."

"Babe, it's on a steel cable. You're clipped onto it. Everything is safe. They do this every day with hundreds of people." He pulled off one of the gloves he had been given to wear and squeezed her shoulder. "It's going to be fun."

"Maybe I should just stay down here." She stepped backward, away from the ladder leading up to the first line. Her backside hit his thighs. "Oh!"

Hunter steadied her. "Careful," he murmured near her ear. He couldn't quite get next to it, since she was wearing a safety helmet. Wishing they were alone, he resolutely shoved away thoughts of how soft and warm and deliciously close to him she was and dropped his hands. "You paid good money to do this. We rode a bus here, you signed a waiver, you put your purse in a locker. You will always regret it if you don't just go for it."

She took a shuddering breath and glanced back at him. "You're right. You're totally right."

He tried not to be amused when she climbed the ladder to the first launching dock as if she was ascending to her own hanging. "Are you afraid of heights?" he asked her when he got to the top behind her. She was clinging to the railing with a death grip.

"No. I don't think so." She glanced over the side. "Maybe."

As the instructor clipped Melanie into the safety gear and had her stand on a platform, he squeezed her gloved hand with his. "It's about letting go, remember? And Celso has you all locked and loaded, right, Celso? Everything is safe."

"We've never lost a single tourist," he assured her.

"There's a first time for everything," she muttered. Her cheeks were flushed.

"Sit down," Celso told her.

Melanie looked at him blankly. "What?"

"Sit down. Just lift your feet and let the rope hold you."

She gave a squeak when she obeyed, and her butt swung back and forth, the harness keeping her dangling there.

"See?" Hunter said. "Going across is no different. You're already letting the rope do all the work. It's the same thing."

Her eyebrows shot up. "Not exactly. Should I close my eyes?"

"No. Eyes wide-open." Then impulsively he leaned over and kissed her. "Have fun."

The instructor gave Melanie a shove, and she took off, screaming at the top of her lungs as she sailed across to the next platform. Hunter winced and shook his head at Celso. "I don't know, man. She may not do the next one."

"She'll be fine," he told him. "Your turn."

It was a fairly tame crossing, and Hunter enjoyed the view of the treetops and the breeze on his face. He dropped onto the other platform and waited for Gil to unhook him so he could gauge Melanie's reaction. She was grinning. Relieved, he told her, "You did it. I knew you could handle it."

"It was scary, but pretty amazing," she said. "To have to trust the rope is hard, but then it was like flying through the air. It was awesome."

"Good." He felt a ridiculous amount of pride that she was enjoying herself. It had nothing to do with him at all, but he wanted her to be happy and to let go. Given that he had encouraged her not to bail, he felt somewhat responsible for her current pleasure.

Speaking of pleasure… He got a great shot of her ass as she stepped up onto the block just a few feet in front of him. He wanted to cup both of those perky cheeks and kiss the back of her neck. An erection started to swell in his cargo shorts, which was not good considering his junk was outlined by the harness. When he glanced up, Gil gave him a knowing glance. Busted. Hunter grinned at the instructor and shrugged his shoulders. The guy gave him a grin back.

Melanie was set to go to the next platform, dangling again. She looked nervous, making an *uh-oh* sound, but at least this time her face had color. When Gil shoved her off the edge she only gave a brief scream before settling into the run. For his turn, Hunter purposely made himself spin, craving a touch more excitement. And a distraction from his hard-on.

She reprimanded him when he landed and was unhooked by Celso, who apparently had run like the wind to get from the previous platform. Hunter was impressed. He was also amused by the dressing-down Melanie gave him.

"Don't do that! You could fall!" She looked indignant and a bit ridiculous, the chin strap on her helmet slightly askew. Her finger came out, the glove too big on her hand. "Don't do that again."

He was touched that she cared enough to be worried he might plunge to his death, especially since he was 100 percent certain there was no way that was going to happen. "Babe, I am not in danger. Trust me." He looked to Celso for confirmation. "Right?"

"Not from the zip line. But anything else, who knows?" was Celso's opinion as he hooked Melanie into the next line.

"Very reassuring," she said.

Hunter reached over and gave her a quick kiss, their helmets knocking a little. "I survived combat. It's all good."

"Is she clear?" he asked Celso.

"Yep. Send her off."

"Don't—"

Melanie looked alarmed, but Hunter just gave her a gentle push, and off she went. Her eyes were wide but then as she settled in she shook her head and gave him a smile. Even better, she started laughing.

Man pride made him grin back at her.

Mission accomplished.

ZIP-LINING HAD BEEN way more fun than Melanie expected. She was pretty damn sure that without Hunter there she would have chickened out entirely. But he'd encouraged and reassured her, and it had been exciting and freeing to sail through the air. She had felt… weightless.

Both physically and emotionally.

Sure, she had been aware that she was wound a little

tight. But she hadn't realized how tense she had been, trying to control her life and her relationship with Ian. The pressure of keeping it a secret and constantly worrying how he felt about her had left her anxious and inflexible. She was pretty sure it had something to do with her failed relationship at seventeen, where she had dived in headfirst with no emotional walls up with a prelaw student her freshman year in college. It had ended in disaster, and she had approached subsequent relationships determined to control them.

Look how well that had turned out.

But a little Mexican sunshine, a sexy bodyguard and a steel cable to dangle from had allowed her to release that anxiety bit by bit, and she felt better than she had in a good long while. Maybe since college and before the heinous breakup, frankly.

After the bus dropped them back in town, she and Hunter wandered around the souvenir shops fingering blankets, dresses, odd trinkets. Hunter pulled on a Mexican wrestling mask, making her laugh hysterically.

"What?" he asked from behind the yellow-and-black-striped rubber. It was too small for his head, so the mouth hole rested on his upper lip, and his chin was exposed. He looked more than a little silly. "I feel like a superhero."

"You really shouldn't." On impulse, she rolled up the bottom of the mask and kissed him full-on. "I prefer you as my bodyguard."

Hunter tore the mask off and tossed it back on the table. "I'm doing a lousy job watching over you from a distance," he said, his voice husky. He pulled her into his arms, her chest brushing against his. "I prefer a more hands-on method, which isn't proper protocol. You should probably fire me."

The now-familiar sensation of arousal washed over her as Hunter brushed his lips over her temple. "I didn't hire you, so I can't fire you."

"Then I quit."

She shivered as he kissed her eyelids, first one then the other. "Is that really necessary?"

"What, you don't want me to quit? You like fraternizing with the help?" He tipped her chin up and kissed her. "Is it exciting?"

She was suddenly overly warm, and it wasn't from the sun beating down on them. "You make me feel exciting," she confessed.

She instantly worried that there was something pathetic about admitting that. As if she were boring and dull and needed him to make her into something interesting.

But Hunter read her emotions and smoothed out her furrowed brow with his fingers. "You are exciting, Melly. You're the most fascinating creature I've ever met because you're sweet and sexy, kind and yet kick-ass. You're everything a man could want."

That was the most wonderful thing any man had ever said to her. It was better than any vow of love or gushing praise for her looks or skills in bed that she'd gotten in the heat of certain moments from boyfriends in the past. This was genuine, matter-of-fact and came from a man who had nothing to gain by flattering her. She was already sleeping with him, and there was a clear understanding between them that it would be nothing more than a vacation fling.

She knew not to read anything into it in terms of a

future, but it was enough to know that he appreciated her. Respected her.

"Thank you, Hunter. That means a lot to me." She dug her fingernails into his shoulders, wanting to grip him solidly, feel his muscles beneath her hands. "You saved this week for me, you know. If you weren't here I would be binge eating and crying. Maybe even drunk texting."

"Well, I'm glad I could save you from that. Nothing worse than an indignant drunk text to make you regret rum the next day."

"No kidding." The thought of sending some kind of "how could you do this to me?" message to Ian was mortifying. But she didn't want to make a joke out of it. "Seriously, thank you."

He fingered the dolphin necklace resting on her chest. "You're welcome." For a second she thought he was going to say something, but then his eyes shuttered. "Anytime."

Was there something there in the way he said that? Melanie wasn't sure, but what she was sure of was that she was having a relaxing vacation, and she owed it to Hunter. She wasn't going to worry about what was happening back in Chicago or about having to return to work. Right now it was impossible to imagine that biting wind and icy sidewalks were waiting for her, and the uncomfortable reality of working for her douchebag ex-boyfriend.

Here it was just warm breezes, hot kisses and living in the moment.

If only she could get Hunter to let go the same way, it would be a perfect vacation.

There was a mariachi band playing in the square,

and the lively beat made her want to swivel her hips and send her skirt twirling. She grabbed his hand. “Dance with me, Hunter.”

He winced. “I don’t think so.”

She laughed. “Come on. I went zip-lining, even though I was scared.”

“I’m not scared. I just don’t want to.” Then he added, “There’s not a lot I’m scared of, Melly.”

“Okay, macho man, duly noted.” It was practically a full-time job dodging his testosterone. It was ridiculous. “What are you scared of, just for future reference?”

She expected him to say snakes or dying or losing his legs. But his eyes darkened.

“Never mind.”

“You can’t *never mind* me,” she murmured, intrigued by his expression. He looked so intense as he stared down at her. “Either tell me or you have to salsa dance with me.”

“I wasn’t aware we were playing truth or dare.”

If that was what it took. “I think we are. Truth or dare, Hunter?”

“Dare,” he said without hesitation.

She wasn’t surprised, but she was slightly disappointed. “Then I guess you’re dancing.”

“I think *we’re* dancing,” he said.

That they were. They were dancing around their feelings about past relationships and about discussing the future. They were attempting to live in the now, which wasn’t all that easy for the majority of human beings. Melanie wasn’t sure she knew the steps to this routine, but she was determined just to close her eyes and follow the beat and enjoy it as best she could.

When they got to the square, she put her arms around Hunter's neck and murmured in his ear, "Move your hips."

"I am."

He was slightly less rigid than a California redwood. "You're barely moving, Hunter."

"Just think of me as a pole, and you can do whatever you want on and around me."

She laughed. "No! That doesn't qualify. And I'm not pole dancing in public."

His eyebrows shot up. "But you will in private?"

About to say no as an automatic response, she paused. "I don't know. Maybe. Depends on the circumstances."

"Figure out those parameters, and I'll make them happen," he said with such sincerity that she laughed again.

But then she realized she wouldn't be seeing him back in Chicago and that he was just teasing her. She would take it as flattery and nothing more. "Be serious," she reprimanded softly. "Distracting me won't get you out of attempting to dance. Here, take my hands."

She held their hands together at their sides and demonstrated how to move her hips. "My foot comes forward, yours goes back. Like this."

She thought he was going to resist and crack another joke. But he concentrated and managed to do an admirable job of moving with her. "See, you've got it."

"You make it easy," Hunter said, his voice husky.

As the music pulsed around them, white fairy lights lit up the night sky and the other couples shimmied, Melanie wondered at how easily she and Hunter had found a rhythm. Together.

12

HUNTER WAS DAMN certain he wouldn't have made a jackass out of himself dancing in public for anyone but Melanie. She seemed to have a way of looking up at him with those limpid eyes and making him agree to just about anything. But he was also glad she had offered him an option between truth and dare. He would rather lob off his own nuts than admit that what he was afraid of was that he was actually falling for her.

As in, he wasn't sure that he could let her disappear entirely from his life once they got back home.

That would be humiliating to admit. One, because it was a stupid thing to be afraid of. He hardly knew her. Two, because the last thing Melanie needed was a guy making her life difficult by placing demands on her right after she got out of a bum relationship. It would be selfish of him to tell her that he wanted to see her again next week, post-Cancún.

Besides, he didn't even know what he meant by that exactly. Did he want to date her? Hang out with her? Just have sex with her? He wasn't sure. He just knew the thought of never seeing her again tied his gut up in knots.

He'd been serious about not wanting a relationship

for a while, if ever. He couldn't do it again—be there for a woman, riding through all her ups and downs while keeping his own feelings to himself, only to have her walk away when she was emotionally satisfied. Over and over again he found himself doing with women what he had done with his mother. He picked them up when they were down, helped them heal, listened to them, gave encouragement. Only to be abandoned once they were on their feet.

In a sense, his mom had done that, too. Every new boyfriend had sucked the majority of her attention; then when things went sour, she was all about her "little man." Hunter had learned to take advantage of those periods in between boyfriends and hoard as much of her affection as possible, squirreling it away, even if that meant most of their time together was spent reassuring her that the ex was a douchebag and that she was beautiful.

He couldn't do that here with Melanie. It was the same damn situation. She was torn up and angry over Ian and did not in any way need him complicating her life. Nor did he need to be left in the dust yet again.

Keep his mouth shut. End of story.

So instead, here he was attempting to dance, and he had to admit that aside from feeling like a *Dancing with the Stars* contestant, and failing, there was something to be said for holding Melanie about the waist and having her smiling and moving in a way that could only be called seductive.

"Let go," she urged him.

He dropped his hands off her waist, confused. "Did I step on you?"

"No. I mean, feel the music."

It was safe to say he had no clue how to do that. "That sounds way too new age for me, Melly, I'm sorry."

"It's like sex," she told him.

That was promising. He waited patiently for her to continue. "Yes?"

"You have to let go like you've been telling me to let go in bed. Let the music sweep you away in pleasure. No thinking. Just feel it."

Hunter had thought Melanie was sexy from the minute he'd met her. But this look she was giving him now was perhaps the hottest expression he'd seen cross her face yet. Because this wasn't her hesitating, or her being coaxed to enjoyment. It was total role reversal, and she was in charge, in command, confident. In her dance moves and otherwise.

"I'm feeling a lot of things," he murmured.

"Oh, yeah? Tell me what those are."

"For starters, once I'm done with this dance, it's my turn to offer you truth or dare."

Her eyebrows shot up. But she just shrugged. "Sure."

Hunter spun her around, catching her off guard. She gave a breathless laugh that died off when he pulled her hard against his chest at the end of the spin. Every man in the square had checked Melanie out at some point or another. Hunter was aware that he was pretty damn lucky that she was with him. He may have slid into this spot by default because Ian Bainbridge was a moron. Didn't mean he was going to enjoy it any less.

"But you're not finished dancing yet," she told him, her fingers gripping the front of his shirt.

"No? Why not?"

"Because you haven't let go yet."

"Have you let go in bed?"

He thought she had, but maybe not as far as it was possible to take it. He was up for seeing just how far he could push her.

"Ninety percent," she said.

He gave her credit for honesty. "I've let go about twenty percent with this dancing. But if you let me take you back to the room, I promise to dance all you want on the veranda."

"It's not the same," she said.

"It will be better." Because then dancing could lead to the horizontal shuffle, and he was all about that while he had the opportunity.

But then someone dancing next to them bumped into their arms, and something about the angle made Hunter's arm explode with pain. It dissipated quickly into a dull ache, but he dropped his hold on Melanie and grimaced.

He expected her to express concern. To mother him the way she had at the zip line place. But she didn't. She just stayed exactly where she was, swaying with him, as though she trusted him to tell her if it was beyond what he could handle. It was that simple gesture, that understanding of what he needed and didn't need, that cracked his reserve. Melanie had gotten under his skin, and maybe wiggled a bit into his heart, he wasn't sure. But he was certain that she deserved him giving her whatever she wanted. That didn't mean a relationship. It just meant a great vacation, and he'd dance like an idiot for that.

The woman wanted hip shaking. He was going to shake it, and then he was going to drop her in a dip so low, he'd literally turn her world upside down.

In fact, she was right. Who gave a shit who was watching or what they thought. He turned Melanie around with one hand and she smiled at him, her skirt flying. When she was back facing him he dropped her down.

She let out a little scream.

He stared into her eyes, getting the distinct impression she wasn't finding this as romantic as he did. Especially when somehow, despite his grip on her, she fell onto the ground.

Oh, God. He'd screwed that up royally. "Maybe we need to work on that move."

At least she was laughing. "That was my fault. My foot slipped." She was struggling to get up.

Hunter held both hands out for her. "You looked beautiful doing it."

She wasn't buying it. "I relent. We can go back to the room."

"Truth or dare?" he asked, giving her a swat on the ass under the pretense of brushing dirt off her as she stood.

"Hey." She swatted at his hand. "Truth."

He should have known that was what she would pick. Though it was fine with him. There was definitely a thing or two he was curious about. "Did you love Ian?" he asked.

Funny enough, he hadn't intended to ask that at all. It just came out, unbidden. He mentally cursed himself. Wow, that was shitty timing.

Her amusement died out. "What? Why?"

"Just answer the question." He'd already asked it, so he had to roll with it, even though he had a feeling it was more revealing than he intended it to be. It almost sounded as though he cared.

Which he did. He hated that Melanie had been hurt and humiliated. It would make it worse if she had truly loved Ian. Frankly, it would also make it harder to continue to have casual sex with her. That felt wrong. He wanted what they were doing to be a free and conscious choice on her part, not an ego stroke or a way to get back at her ex.

She stared up at him, her tongue sliding along her bottom lip, wetting it. Slowly, her head went back and forth. "No. I didn't love Ian. I guess that makes me a terrible person, doesn't it?"

His instant relief was quickly replaced by confusion. "What? Why would you say that? Of course not."

Melanie started walking in the direction of their resort, and he took her hand in his, wanting to touch her, feel the warmth of her body near his. He felt protective of her, and it had nothing to do with being her bodyguard. Which he wasn't. Not really.

"Because I was with him even though I didn't love him."

That was some kind of female logic he didn't quite grasp. "Melly, no one starts a relationship in love. That grows as you move forward after the initial attraction. If we all threw in the towel at four weeks or something like that, we'd be in a revolving door of relationships."

"I guess. But it seems as though I should have loved him by that point."

Now he was really mystified. "But he's a douchebag. Why would you love a douchebag?"

"That's not the point."

He'd learned that even if he didn't know what the

hell a woman's point was, he should never admit it. Just make a noncommittal sound and move on. "Hmm. Do you want to get a taxi?"

"No, I'm fine walking. As long as you think it's safe."

"I'm sure it's safe. We're on a main drag, and we're in a tourist area."

"Okay. So truth or dare?"

Hold up. "Wait, we're doing a second round?"

"Of course. You never do it just once. What's the fun in that?"

"Fair enough." He was feeling ballsy. "Truth."

She looked surprised. "Did you love your girlfriend?"

Yikes. His own question turned back on him. "I think that's breaking the rules. You asked me the same question I asked you."

"No, I didn't. I didn't ask you if you loved Ian." She gave him a smirk.

"Hey, now. Getting a little sassy, aren't you?" But he liked it. He liked that she was feeling comfortable and confident with him.

"Just answer the question. Or I'll be forced to give you dare—and that will have you swimming naked with the dolphins tonight at midnight."

Yep. Sassy. "Playing hardball now, huh? Fine. I will answer the question. No, I didn't love Danielle. I cared about her. I enjoyed her company, and I respected her as a person."

That sounded…professional. But it was the truth. He didn't think it was particularly unusual to be with someone under those circumstances. They had never lied to each other and made promises. There had been mutual admiration and companionship. Not bad things to base a romance on.

Romance. What an odd word. He wasn't sure he even understood what it meant.

"But you wanted to be with her."

"Yes. Because I was willing to ignore warning signs. When I met her, she was out of a bad relationship, and she needed to talk about it a lot. So things started out with her sharing feelings, not asking about me, and then it frustrated her that I didn't share as much as she wanted."

"What I don't understand is why she would just suddenly dump you when you got home. Why wait like that?"

"Maybe she liked the idea of having someone, of being able to say she had a boyfriend who was deployed, but the reality didn't live up to whatever she'd been expecting when I was gone." Did it matter? He wasn't sure it did. "Whatever the hell happened, I don't totally understand it. What I do understand is I'm not in a position to have a relationship right now."

"Clearly neither am I," she murmured. "I'm like Danielle, aren't I? On the rebound, letting you comfort me."

It was pretty obvious to both of them that was exactly what was going on. It wasn't a bad thing. It just wasn't anything to base a future on beyond Cancún, even if either of them thought they might want that. Which he wasn't sure they did.

"There's nothing wrong with that, Melly. Don't feel guilty. We're enjoying each other. It's not one-sided." He was enjoying her, no doubt about it. "For the record, when you were taking me into your mouth, I did not feel as though I was comforting you."

"Good. That was about you." She stared up at him with deep, seductive eyes. "Sad thing is, I couldn't stay away from you right now if I tried."

"So don't."

They were approaching the resort, and it was lit up, spotlights shining on the glossy white building. There was music coming faintly from somewhere, and the sound of the ocean waves crashing onto the beach directly behind the building. It seemed odd to Hunter that the sound of the ocean could supersede all the volume produced by the humans inside the building. But nature had a way of dominating, despite man's best intentions otherwise.

As Hunter stood there, pausing in front of the hotel, he decided he wanted to skirt the building entirely and take Melanie for a walk on the beach.

Romance was like the ocean. It superseded all the noise created by life.

He wanted to give Melanie romance.

She deserved it.

Hell, maybe he needed to give it as much as she needed to receive it. Hadn't they both been in relationships based on logic and proximity and basic compatibility instead of passion and love? He didn't want to give her advice or a shoulder to cry on. He wanted to give both of them total escape: from the snow, from the past, from loneliness.

Hunter leaned over and kissed Melanie, taking her mouth in a rough, dominating kiss because he needed to taste her, feel her lips beneath his. "Was that comforting?"

“Not particularly.” Her voice was a low whisper. “More like arousing.”

“Good.” He stroked her cheek with his thumb. “I don’t want you to feel as though I’m taking advantage of your breakup.”

“I don’t,” she protested. “This is mutual.”

“Then, don’t say this is about me comforting you. It’s about forgetting all the shit that drags us down at home. It’s about here. Now. You, me, warm water and soft sand. Our skin touching. That’s all.” And that was everything.

“I was wrong,” she said. “You’re not like James Bond at all. You’re much more eloquent.”

That was flattering enough that it made him uncomfortable. So instead of acknowledging it, he said, “Let’s go down here first,” tugging her in the direction of the path that led to the beach.

“Are you trying to get out of the veranda dance you promised?” she asked, looking at him suspiciously, but letting him lead her.

Well, yes, but that had no bearing on his decision. “No, of course not. I just thought it would feel good to dip our toes in the ocean.”

She gave a sigh of pleasure. “It would, wouldn’t it? I can’t believe we haven’t even lain on the beach yet.”

“Do you have any more excursions planned?” He hoped not, in all honesty. The zip-lining had been fun, the horseback riding awful, and now he just wanted to spend the rest of the week relaxing with Melanie. Eating his weight in seafood and fresh mangoes.

“The Mayan ruins on Friday.”

Under other circumstances, he was all about a little history and culture. But he had a feeling this was going to involve a bumpy bus ride and strangers wanting to chat with him while joking about needing a *cerveza*. He was craving privacy. "That sounds interesting."

"We can probably cancel."

He must not have sounded enthusiastic. There was no way he wanted his opinion to influence her. Pushing a giant banana leaf back so they could continue on the path, passing an endless row of patios off hotel rooms, he immediately tried to reassure her. "No, of course not. I mean, if you want to, that's fine, and obviously you must want to if you signed up to do it."

"The water there is supposed to be really blue."

That was a baffling statement to him. "Melly, the water *here* is really blue."

She laughed. "Yes, but I thought with the ruins jutting up, and the water as the background, it would make great photos."

Ah. So that was it. Maybe she didn't really care that much about seeing the ruins herself. She had thought it would make Ian happy. The ungrateful bastard.

"Probably. We don't have to decide tonight. We can go and ask tomorrow if it's even possible to get a refund. If not, then we should just go. I'm sure we'll enjoy it." Then to make her laugh, he added, "Or die trying."

She made a sound of amusement. "Isn't that what vacation is about?"

They were at the edge of the hotel, about to step down onto the beach. He stopped and turned back to gather Melanie in his arms. "No. This is what vacation is about." He brushed her blond hair off her cheek and bent to brush his lips tenderly across hers. "It's about pleasure."

He had to admit to himself it was also about companionship. Easy, simple companionship.

It was amazing what a few days could do. Instead of looking at her with pure lust, those feelings were now intermingled with something more. Deeper. He had genuine affection for her, and he wasn't sure what in the hell he was supposed to do with that back in Chicago. But there was tonight.

He caressed her cheek with his thumb while he took her mouth again, enjoying the soft sigh she gave as she succumbed to his kiss. They tasted and touched, his tongue dipping into her open mouth. Everything about Melanie turned him on, from the way she smelled to that soft little sigh she gave between kisses. She was sensual and beautiful and generous, and he held her tighter, wanting to remember this moment. Remember her.

When her arms came up to snake around his neck, he was suddenly overcome by the need to take her right there, right then. The end of the path was private, the beach on one side, and a retaining wall with bushes on the other. If he walked her behind the hedge, no one would hear a thing.

The thought was a total turn-on. The perfect way to get Melanie to totally let go. "Back up," he urged her, walking forward so she was forced to step back.

"What? Why?"

"I want to kiss you in private." Okay, that was something of a con, but he did want more privacy.

The look she gave him indicated she didn't buy it. "I thought we were going for a walk."

"We are. We're walking five feet behind you." He

brushed his fingers over her nipples through her sundress.

She sucked in her breath sharply.

"Let me kiss you. Please." He was asking for more, and they both knew it.

Her sandals made a sound in the gravel as she took two steps back, watching him carefully, her breasts heaving in the moonlight. "Kiss me, Hunter. Everywhere."

It would be his pleasure.

IT WAS DARK on the secluded edge of the path, but Melanie could see Hunter's nostrils flare. She knew what he was asking, and he knew that she had just agreed. Maybe he didn't want to actually take it beyond making out, but even that was hard for her to do in a setting like this. It required acquiescence to the moment, to the desire. She wasn't good at that. It went against her control-freak personality, and Hunter knew that, but there was something about him. He made her feel soft without feeling vulnerable. Sexy without feeling like an object. He made her let her hair down, literally and figuratively, and laugh. She felt feminine, confident, desirable, appreciated.

That was it. She felt *appreciated* by Hunter. Something she hadn't felt in who knew how long.

So she let him lead her, moving forward with a determined expression so she was forced to back up until she hit the wall. That soft thump of her back on the stucco tripped off a ripple of desire, starting from her core and easing out into all her limbs. There was no retreat. Hunter was going to touch her, and she was going to submit to him. It was exciting, arousing. His hand landed low on her waist, his thumb stroking over the apex of her thigh. His other hand cupped her breast, and he teased at her nipple.

She anticipated his lips on hers, but instead his tongue flicked across her bottom lip, and she arched toward him, a craving for more igniting deep inside her. He knew how to expertly tease her to greater pleasure. When he sucked her moist flesh into his mouth gently several times, her head dropped back and her eyes drifted shut. "Hunter," she murmured. She wanted more.

Without even realizing she had done it, she had wrapped her leg around him and was grinding her hips against his. She could feel his erection pressing into her, but the angle was such that it wasn't any sort of relief, it was only teasing and antagonizing. His answer to her pleading was to pinch her nipple at the same time his tongue plunged into her mouth. It was pure, sweet torture, and she moaned into him, gripping his shoulders tightly.

Before Hunter, she had been aware of her body, obviously, but not like this. Not like this understanding and consciousness of every inch of her flesh, and all its curves and dips and ways she could feel alive. He could make her shiver with just a brushing over her inner thighs. He did that as he took her mouth, skirting her clitoris over and over with his touch, making her feel more and more desperate for solid contact. When he finally slipped his hand under her skirt, blocking her from anyone's view with his solid frame, she was grateful to finally feel his strokes without the barrier of her cotton sundress. But he still didn't give her the relief she wanted; he didn't shift her panties to the side.

He just kissed her over and over until she was weak in the knees, damp with desire, breathing hard, totally unaware of the hard wall behind her back.

All she was aware of was him and her own body.

The ocean waves were creating a white noise humming in the distance, and the air was warm, her body even more so.

When he finally slipped a finger under her panties and into her moist arousal, she moaned louder than she had intended. For a second she was embarrassed, glancing around his shoulders to see if anyone was around, but then he shifted his mouth onto the swell of her breast at the same time his thumb stroked over her clitoris. This time when she groaned she didn't care who heard her. That felt *good.*

"Yeah?" he asked.

She nodded and managed to answer, "Yes." It was so amazing that she couldn't prevent herself from rocking onto his finger repeatedly. She found a faster and faster rhythm, losing herself to the moment.

But then Hunter stilled her hips by pressing her back against the wall. She gave a cry of disappointment.

He shifted her dress a little higher and tugged her panties down. They fell to her ankles, and she realized where this was going. Part of her, the efficient, organized, uptight Melanie, balked inside. The other part, the one who felt alive with Hunter, didn't let the uptight side of her have an opinion. So she sagged, letting the wall hold her up, and gave herself to the moment. Gave herself to Hunter.

When he surged into her, she was ready for him, open and eager.

Two strokes and she found her release, already so

primed by him it was all it took. She bit her lip to keep from making too much noise and hung on to him with white knuckles.

Hunter followed her just a few minutes later, and for a long moment they just stared at each other, still intimately connected, breathing hard.

Finally, he pulled back. "Damn." Dropping into a squat, he eased her panties back up into place, kissing her inner thigh as he did. Then he dropped her dress back down over her. "All that needed was a waterfall to be the hottest thing ever."

"That probably would have killed me," she told him sincerely.

He laughed and leaned over and kissed her forehead. "Me, too." He tugged her off the wall. "Now, how about that walk on the beach?"

"Only if I don't need my legs." She wasn't sure she had bucolic strolling in her at this point. Her thighs were actually shaking.

"Truth or dare," he asked, ignoring her reluctance. He tucked her hair behind her ear.

"Doesn't that count retroactively as a dare?"

"What does?"

"What we just did." She felt as though she was blushing, or maybe it was just the warm flush of their heated exchange and her climax.

"No, that doesn't count. I didn't ask you truth or dare before we started."

"Fine. Truth." He was propelling her along with a firm grip on her hand. The minute their feet hit the sand, though, Melanie was glad he had persisted. "Ah, that feels good."

"It does. But no avoiding the question. What's the best sex you've ever had?"

Melanie froze. She couldn't answer that. Because the truth was it was the sex they had been having. Not one moment, or one orgasm, but the collective vacation affair they had been sharing.

But surely that would sound pathetic. That the best sex in her life was with a guy she'd just met, who had been paid to protect her. A little more revealing than she would like it to be, so she wasn't going to let on. Not yet.

"I don't know," she hedged. "Let me think about it."

The one thing she did know was that what she and Hunter had done was going to be a blueprint for her future sex life.

Hunter kicked off his sandals and sank to the sand in a quiet and private spot just beyond the grassy area of the resort. He pulled her down next to him. They could see a few people down by the water. The night air was still warm, but there was a chill to it without the sun. It would have been relaxing except that she was trying to formulate a response for Hunter that wasn't a flat-out lie. She'd chosen *truth*, and she was a rule follower, plain and simple. There was nothing wrong with that, but it was inconvenient at times.

"Is your sexual history so extensive, then?" he joked.

Melanie knew Hunter enough to know that he joked when he wasn't sure what to say, so it reassured her that he wasn't 100 percent comfortable with his question, either. She wondered why he had asked it.

Maybe it was because he wanted it to be the very answer she was afraid to give.

"Well, you know, I've built a film career on it," she teased back.

That made him laugh. "I'd almost forgotten, Ms. Ambrosia."

They could leave it at that. Or she could expose herself totally to him.

He had seen her at her most vulnerable; he had been there when she'd gotten dumped by correspondence—one of the most awkward and embarrassing moments she'd ever had. And that had only been the beginning. Now she had truly let loose, and had had a quickie with him behind a hedge. She was open to him whether she had intended to be or not.

Then she realized that thinking about it in terms of weights and balances was the wrong approach. Hunter wasn't a cruel man. He wasn't going to use her words against her. What did it matter if she told him the truth? The only way to truly let go and enjoy a moment, or in this case a week, was to stop hiding behind emotional walls and throw it all out there.

So with her toes in the sand and Hunter's hand in hers, she stroked her thumb over the callused skin on the back of his hand. "I guess I have the average amount of experience for a twenty-eight-year-old woman. A few noteworthy partners from serious relationships, a few encounters that were less serious, one debacle."

"Yeah, that does sound about right."

"So based on that, I would say the best sex I've ever had is with you." Then she added a caveat just in case it was too heavy for him, or gave him the impression she wanted more. "I mean, in terms of casual sex. Sex outside of a relationship."

For a second he didn't say anything. His jaw was tense in profile as she watched him. "I wasn't fishing for a compliment. I wanted to know what you've enjoyed the most so I can repeat it for you. Give me your favorite position."

"Oh." Melanie refused to feel awkward or as if she had said too much. She was going to expand her statement, explain to him that everything he did had a delicious effect on her. But Hunter kept speaking.

"But before you tell me how much you love to be on top, I need to tell you something."

"What?" Those words made her nervous. His head turned, and the intensity of his stare took her breath away.

"Sex with you is fantastic. I love the way you smell and the way you taste and the way you sound. I love the way you come apart in my arms, Melly."

She would come apart for him anytime.

Melanie laid her head on Hunter's shoulder. "I think your girlfriend was wrong. You do a pretty damn good job of sharing your feelings."

Hunter put his arm around her. "Sharing my feelings isn't an issue if someone is willing to listen."

Her heart swelled. "I'll listen. I'm a good listener. You can say whatever you want."

His lips brushed her temple. "All I really want to say right now is that you're beautiful, and I'm glad the firm put me on this assignment. There isn't anywhere else in the world I'd rather be."

The sand, the surf, the hottest guy in the world telling her she was beautiful.

Best vacation ever.

13

HUNTER STARED AT the water, wondering, even as he was enjoying every second with Melanie, if this had been a mistake. He wasn't sure he could stay removed, casual about her. When she had looked him in the eye and said she would listen, he had believed her. For the first time in a good long while, he felt as if he'd met a woman who wanted to give to him just as much, if not more than she wanted to take.

It was utterly tempting and such a bad, awful, wrong idea.

Her head rested on his shoulder, and he felt protective of her. Totally, ridiculously enamored.

Was it a bad idea?

Yes. Because one or both of them would get hurt, and the last thing in the world he wanted to do was hurt Melanie.

Her fingers snaked through his until they were holding hands, and he couldn't help but kiss the top of her head again. His chest tightened. This wasn't just sex. He was feeling things that were beyond just wanting to have a little bit of fun. He felt invested in her. He loved to see her smile, and he felt at ease around her. He wanted to find out what it would be like to see Melanie back home. Take her out to dinner, see a movie, go to the opening-day ball game in April.

Which was dating. After he'd just sworn he wasn't going to get into another relationship. How messed up was he?

He needed to keep his damn mouth shut. He had been the one who'd insisted they agree to casual Cancún sex, and she had been on board with that. He couldn't suddenly spring on her that maybe he wanted to see if they could extend their time together. Because what did that really mean anyway?

It was like bait and switch. He'd promised her no strings, and now he wanted something different. It wasn't fair.

"Can we head back?" Melanie asked. "I know it's ridiculous to say this, but I'm getting chilly."

Relieved to have his thoughts interrupted he said, "That is ridiculous. Come on, little miss sunshine." He stood and held out his hand to help her up.

"If you could live anywhere in the world, where would you live?" Melanie asked him as she rose to her full height.

That was a question he hadn't really asked himself. "I don't know. Key West? Somewhere warm and laid-back where I don't have to wear a suit."

"But you look so sexy in a suit."

He liked that. "Do I? Thanks." As they walked toward their room he asked, "What about you? Where would you live?"

"Somewhere warm." She laughed. "I love Chicago, I really do. But my body can't take it."

"What can your body take?" he asked.

She caught the shift in tone. "I can think of a thing or two."

"I can think of five or six."

Yet Melanie was yawning repeatedly, and when they got into the room she stretched, sighed and disappeared into the bathroom. When she came out she was wearing her hair up, her face shiny and clean. Before he could blink or come on to her, she was out of her sundress and into pajamas.

Pajamas were dumb. They were a barrier between him and her, and that made him grumpy.

"Let's just cuddle," she said.

Cuddling was nice. If you were a panda. But he supposed he had to leave her the hell alone at some point.

She slipped into bed. "Ah. Cool sheets. The best thing ever."

Not by a mile. Hunter stripped down to his underwear and climbed in beside her. She wriggled over and managed to adhere every inch of herself to every inch of him in a way that wasn't sexual. It was a talent. He wouldn't have even thought it was possible to be touching *everywhere* and not be having sex. Her head was on his shoulder, her fingers on his chest, stroking him so lightly it almost tickled.

It was nice. He had to admit it. He'd forgotten how relaxing it could be to share physical space with someone and hold them with zero agenda. Wrapping his arm around Melanie's back, he kissed the messy topknot on her head.

As she affectionately kissed his chest and stroked his abs, as if it was second nature to her, as if they did this all the time, Hunter gradually relaxed, muscle by muscle, even as warning bells went off in his head.

You didn't do this with a casual lover. Probably not even with a friend with benefits. They were crossing a line they shouldn't cross. Yet he liked it and didn't want it to end.

His eyes started to drift closed. "Mmm, that feels good," he told her, so she wouldn't stop caressing him.

"You feel good. Good night, Hunter."

"Night, Melanie." He leaned over and turned the light off.

As they lay there in the dark, he realized that she had managed to achieve something rather extraordinary—she had both coaxed him out of a bad mood and gotten him to relax. Open up. All by just being herself. Smiling. Touching him.

He had let go, too.

He really should be terrified by what that meant, but instead he just felt…pleased.

It didn't even annoy him when the dolphins kept waking him up with their nocturnal shenanigans. They were definitely party animals. Hell, maybe dolphins never slept. He was no marine biologist. He had no clue how Melanie was sleeping through it, but given how even and steady her breath was, she seemed to be doing just fine.

Until finally she said, "If they don't shut up in the next sixty seconds, I'm going to strangle them with my necklace."

Hunter laughed. "I didn't even know you were awake."

With a sigh, she opened her eyes. "No one could possibly sleep through Splish and Splash out there. What are they doing?"

"I have no idea, but whoever had the brilliant idea to stick them outside the hotel rooms should be fired."

"Agreed. Maybe if we turn on the TV it will drown them out?"

"Worth a shot." Hunter groped around in the dark for the remote and found it on the nightstand. He hit Power and immediately a bright image appeared on the screen, making him squint.

Then squint again.

"Uh…"

It was porn. A very naked man and a very naked woman were getting it on, and the English subtitles at the bottom made it clear they were both enjoying it.

Melanie started laughing. "This needs subtitles? Oh, my God."

"That's what she said." Hunter changed the channel, but every single one was in Spanish. "Do you speak Spanish?"

"No."

"Me, either." He returned the remote to the nightstand. "Want to go out on the veranda? If we have to suffer the dolphins, at least there's a warm breeze and a hammock outside."

"Sure."

They climbed out of bed. Melanie glanced at him. "Are you going to get dressed?"

"I don't see why. The dolphins aren't." He was already being forced out of bed. He wasn't shoving himself back into shorts. "Besides, I have underwear on."

Melanie gave him a dubious look. "They don't cover a whole lot."

Then she shocked him by reaching out and sliding a hand across his ass.

"Hey, now," he said as he opened the door to the veranda. "I think that rather suggestive TV show inspired you."

She rolled her eyes, but even in the moonlight he could see her cheeks turn pink. Melanie was easy to tease.

She was also easy to hold. Hunter got in the hammock and pulled her into his arms. The fit was as perfect as it had been on the bed. "Ah. This is better. We can hear the ocean."

Hunter glanced over to study Melanie's cute nose, her plump, soft lips and her pink cheeks. She looked healthy, alive. Maybe it was the sun earlier that day; maybe it was being on vacation. But she looked as though she was glowing.

"Don't move," he said, climbing out of the hammock and popping back into the room. He returned a moment later with his cell phone in hand and fiddled with it, finding the camera button. He wanted a picture of her like this. No filter.

"What are you doing?"

"Taking your picture." He expected her to protest, but she didn't. He held the phone up and steadied his hand, making sure the screen displayed mostly her face. "You look beautiful." Happy. She looked happy. He felt insanely proud of that fact. Not that it was his doing, per se. But he wasn't making her unhappy, like Ian had. That was a victory in his estimation. That it mattered so much to him was unnerving.

"Thanks. I feel very peaceful." She sighed and rubbed a little against him. "Take one of us so I can remember this moment when I'm stressed back home dodging snow plows."

"I can do that." He hit the camera button again and positioned his arm so they were both on screen. What he saw made his heart damn near skip a beat. They looked…together. Like a couple. Easy and comfortable with each other.

He hit the button several times, wanting to capture the intimacy of their embrace. Melanie didn't smile with her teeth, but just gave the camera a sweet smile. Then he turned and glanced at her while he hit the button again. He wanted to look at them later. See her. See him with her. Hunter kissed her.

They didn't speak, just held each other, the weightlessness of the hammock soothing, the distant lull of the ocean making Hunter's eyes drift closed.

HUNTER WENT TO the ruins with Melanie. She knew he really didn't want to, but he never said a word. After two days of lying on the beach and splashing in the ocean together, she was more relaxed than she could have imagined possible, and she was enjoying their day poking around the crumbling ruins. Hunter was sitting on the edge of a cliff, his feet dangling over the side, his head turned up toward the sun, eyes closed.

She clearly wasn't the only one who had needed this vacation. Hunter seemed more and more open and at ease with her. He had talked about his mother, who sounded like a pistol, and about how he would like to get a dog. Music, movies, sports… They had covered the basic ground when getting to know someone, and as she stared at him, the majestic ocean turquoise blue behind him, she realized that if she went home and never saw him again, there would be a hole in her heart.

Maybe they could be friends, or maybe only lovers

or maybe something more, but what she had learned this week was that she no longer wanted to play it safe. In shielding her heart, she had only managed to hurt it. So if she wanted a real shot at happiness with a man, she needed to stop standing back from the edge. She needed to dangle over the edge like Hunter's feet were right now.

So she went and sat down next to him. "Hey, stranger."

He opened one eye. "Hey, sexypants."

That made her laugh. "Melly Sexypants is almost a better stage name than Melly Ambrosia."

"No one would take you seriously if that was your name," he deadpanned.

His hand snaked over and landed on her knee, massaging her skin below her sundress.

"Do we have to go home?" she asked.

"I'm down with running away if you are."

Melanie figured now was the time. Throw it out there. Otherwise what would happen? If she waited one more night, then suddenly they'd be on the plane, and the whole damn thing would be awkward. It would be too late. They would go their separate ways, him establishing his place in the security firm and her dealing with the fallout of her dead relationship with Ian.

"Unfortunately, I like to eat and have a roof over my head."

"That is somewhat important," he agreed.

God, she was losing her nerve. "But I was thinking… maybe when we get back home, we can see each other again. You know, let go for real. Live in the moment."

Her heart thumped unnaturally fast in her chest as she waited for him to answer.

Hunter's expression was shuttered. "We talked about this. I thought we decided it wouldn't be a good idea."

Even as her heart sank, she forged ahead, not ready to back down until she spoke all her feelings honestly. "Did we? We agreed it was a vacation fling. We didn't talk about why we could or couldn't see each other back in Chicago."

"I don't want to hurt you."

"Why would you hurt me?" she asked, honestly curious. "You didn't hurt Danielle. She hurt you."

"I don't know that I'm *enough* for you."

"Let me decide that. Let's just hang out and see what happens."

"Sex, that's what will happen." He turned to her, and his eyes were intense, his jaw shut. "And we'll spend all our time together, and then I'm going to end up falling for you."

"I would like that," she said simply. "Because I've already fallen for you."

There was a pause. "What about Ian?"

"What about him?" This had absolutely nothing to do with Ian, other than the fact that he was an example of how she wasn't taking enough risks when it came to men. She needed to leap, stop playing it safe and settling.

"You work for him."

It wasn't a question, and Melanie nodded. "Yes. Are you afraid I'm going to get back together with him?"

"I don't know." He sounded grumpy. "See, that's what you would have to deal with. Me not being able to articulate my feelings."

She kissed his shoulder. "You've been a friend to me. I don't want you to disappear as suddenly from my life as you appeared. You can share or not share whatever you want with me."

Melanie searched his face when he didn't respond. "You want to know my feelings? I want you to quit your job. I want you to march into that office and tell Bainbridge to suck it. He shouldn't be allowed to do what he did to you and not think there are consequences."

She appreciated his indignation on her behalf, but he was forgetting something. "The only person who is punished if I quit is me. Ian will just hire a replacement."

"I doubt it's that simple."

"It is." Her throat felt tight at the thought. "I do what hundreds of people are qualified to do. It doesn't make any sense to quit without another position in place."

"So find another position."

Melanie frowned. "Why does it matter?"

"I want you to be valued, respected." He leaned over and kissed her softly. "I don't understand how Bainbridge didn't see how amazing you are."

Her heart softened. "Funny. I've been thinking the same thing about your ex-girlfriend all week."

"I get it, though. I'm sorry. I can't expect you to quit your job out of pure righteousness. But I do think you'd be happier if you found something new."

"I'll give it some thought. Thanks for worrying about me." She appreciated it, but she wasn't sure she had a lot of options.

Hunter brushed his thumb over her bottom lip, and she leaned closer to him. "I think we are dating, aren't we?" he asked. "I mean, I think every day we've been inching in that direction."

"I agree. I think we are dating."

"We're insane."

Determined not to let that be a deterrent for either of them, she nudged his leg with hers. "No. Insane would be me pushing you off this cliff."

He laughed. "That would be a twist no one saw coming."

Melanie wrapped her arms around his neck. "I think I've had enough twists for one week. I think I'd like to just hold on to you for a while, if that's okay."

"It's more than okay."

14

"I CAN'T BELIEVE we're going back to reality," Melanie said, fingering her dolphin necklace as she and Hunter sat in the airport in Cancún waiting for their flight to board. She was feeling a multitude of emotions. Gratitude to Hunter for saving her vacation from disaster. Satisfaction that she had genuinely relaxed, let go, enjoyed herself. But also fear that once she got home it was all going to evaporate in the grind of the everyday. Fear, too, of having to go to Bainbridge Studios and face Ian's nonchalance.

Hunter was playing with his phone and didn't even glance up at her. He had put on his suit for the flight home, and it was an intriguing juxtaposition of day one and the intervening days. Now they were full circle, but back to what?

"Every day can't be a holiday," he said.

Thanks, Captain Obvious. Melanie mentally rolled her eyes. Of course she knew that. But she was seeking a little bit of reassurance. Men never seemed to understand that she had an internal dialogue going on in her head. She knew how she wanted a man to respond before he even spoke. Which was irrational and unfair, she realized, but that didn't stop her from wanting Hunter to understand what she was asking.

"Where do you live?" she asked. It had suddenly occurred to her that they might be an hour apart. Not that she supposed it mattered. They were probably only going to see each other occasionally.

"Lincoln Park. You?"

"Wrigleyville."

He was still studying his phone. She told herself to shut up. Just be quiet and worry in silence. Because this was her issue, not his. Hunter had been up front with her. He had been solicitous, sexy, kind. She didn't want to ruin the tail end of a fabulous week with her own neuroses when she was the one who had suggested they continue seeing each other. But the problem with being a control freak was she wanted to efficiently cross items off her checklist. Dating Hunter—check. But relationships didn't work like that. She needed to calm the hell down and let it roll. See where it went.

Hunter rolled his shoulder, raising his arm up and down a few times to loosen it up. "I'm going to get a beer. You want anything?"

"No, I'm good." She was just going to sit there and chew her manicure off.

After he stood up, he leaned back down and gave her a soft kiss. "Stop worrying. There isn't anything you can't handle when you get back."

Hunter had a way of forcing her out of herself and making her relax. She actually felt her shoulders release at his words. "Thanks. You're right."

When he walked away in pursuit of beer, she watched him. His gait was strong, confident. Sexy. He was gorgeous and thoughtful. She had seen and touched every inch of him, and he'd done the same to her. She wasn't ready to let go of him. There was more fun to be had, and she hoped he genuinely felt the same way.

They had spent their last few days on the beach, body surfing, lying in the sun, reading. Making love at night for hours until they were both exhausted and satisfied on every level. Melanie wondered if she had become too attached. If she was expecting something from Hunter that he couldn't give her, like he had suggested.

What did she want, exactly?

Her phone dinged in her bag, and she pulled it out. Hunter had forwarded her the hammock pictures from a couple nights earlier. It amazed her how flushed and glassy eyed she looked in them. As if she was content on every level.

But even more startling was the one where Hunter was gazing at her.

That one took her breath away.

His lips were turned up in a soft smile, and he leaned toward her, as though he couldn't possibly get close enough.

Was this what casual sex looked like?

Somehow she didn't think so.

She wasn't just getting attached to Hunter—she was falling in love with him.

The realization robbed her of her breath. She'd gone and fallen in love with her bodyguard turned temporary lover.

But she couldn't help it. They had spent over six straight days together, in each other's company almost every minute. They had talked, laughed; he had reassured her, comforted her, encouraged her. She had done things she wouldn't have been able to do without him, from zip-lining to really exploring her sexual freedom.

She had opened herself up to him, and what had sprung from that were feelings she in no way expected. It was nuts to fall in love with a man she had only known for a week. But maybe when you stripped the real world away and spent time with someone in close proximity, you stopped playing games. You stopped shielding yourself from disappointment. You let down all your defenses and really got to know the person. The real him.

It was that Hunter that had captured her heart.

It was the Hunter that, despite her saying she didn't want anything, brought a banana back with him.

"They don't feed us on the plane," he said by way of explanation as he handed her the fruit. He winked. "And I know what you can do to a banana. If it's not your favorite, it's certainly mine."

That made her laugh, worries temporarily eased. He was good for her. There was no doubt about it.

"Thanks." She put the banana in her lap.

He eyed her crotch and raised his eyebrows up and down.

Hunter would think she was insane if she told him she was in love with him. He'd run for the hills. Refuse to board the plane with her.

Or maybe he would say he felt the same way.

Their boarding call was announced, and Hunter held his hand out to her with a smile. "Let's go," he said.

She couldn't do it. She couldn't tell him.

Apparently, she hadn't entirely learned how to let go on this vacation. She couldn't make herself that vulnerable and risk having him recoil from her. At least not before a three-hour flight home.

So she took his hand and smiled, but stayed silent. It was all about timing. She'd know when it was right to tell him more about how she felt. This wasn't a cop-out. It was playing the game strategically.

After takeoff, Hunter encouraged her to lay her head down on his lap so she could stretch out. Staring up at him, she smiled. "What are your plans for the rest of the weekend?" she asked, as a not-so-subtle attempt to have him suggest they do something together.

The corner of his mouth tilted up as though he knew exactly what she was getting at. "Whatever you're doing."

That worked for her. It was a little late to play coy, but she still teased, "Oh. I was just planning to do some laundry."

"What do you need clothes for?" Then his eyes widened and his nostrils flared, which she recognized as his shift into sexy thoughts. "You can open the door for me wearing high-heeled boots and a winter coat and nothing else."

Oh, yeah, he was going there. She felt the evidence of it growing right next to her ear. Melanie sat up, flustered in a good way. "I'm sure that can be arranged. How about dinner, tomorrow night, my place?"

She'd ply him with risotto and merlot and Melly moves, and then months from now, if they were still dating, she would reinvestigate the whole issue of whether or not she was truly in love with him.

Having a plan made her feel better.

Everything was easier with a plan.

It completely defeated the purpose of letting go on

vacation, putting her emotions in the same lockbox they'd occupied for the past decade, but it was forward progress of some sort. In a manner of speaking.

Melanie turned on her phone after they'd landed. It was the first time she'd checked it in a week, and she found dozens of emails along with a number of texts, including one from Ian sent several days earlier.

I'm sorry.

That was it. Just a generic apology.

As she parted ways with Hunter at the taxi queue with a brief kiss, she wondered grimly if playing it safe was going to land her in the same position all over again. Nothing had changed in her life, and it was deflating.

It was sleeting outside. Cold, icy water along with a winter wind pelted her in the face as she climbed out of the cab in front of her apartment building.

Melanie suddenly wasn't sure about anything. She kept asking herself what she wanted, and she honest to God didn't know the answer. And she didn't know how to find out.

IF HUNTER HAD known he wasn't going to see Melanie for five days, he would have given her a better kiss as they parted ways at the airport. He had been expecting a full weekend with her, but en route to his apartment he'd gotten a call from his boss. He had put him on a job for Saturday and Sunday, which Hunter wasn't in any position to refuse, and then once the workweek had started Melanie had been occupied with other plans—something with a girlfriend Monday evening and a work event on Tuesday. So here it was Wednesday at eight o'clock at night, and he was just taking the stairs to her apartment to see her for the first time.

He wasn't going to lie. He felt both excited to see her and uncomfortable. It was different being back home. There was no mariachi band, no bikinis, no fruity cocktails. There was just work, a relentless winter and no real knowledge of each other beyond vacation time. They hadn't even talked on the phone. Just texts. Hunter felt with each day that passed there was a distance growing between them, removing bit by bit the ease they'd felt together. There had been a lot of thinking time, and in those days he had wondered yet again if dating Melanie now was a mistake. Shouldn't she be taking some time and making sure this was what she wanted instead of diving into dating him a hot minute after her breakup?

When Melanie opened her door to him, she looked as uneasy as he felt. "Hi," she said softly, her smile tentative. "Come on in. Do you want some wine?"

"Um, sure." He didn't want wine, but what the hell? He kicked off his slushy boots and followed her down the narrow hallway. Her apartment was small and cozy, but lacking in personality in a way he hadn't expected. It was very beige and neutral. "I can open the bottle for you."

"I've got it." She gave a little laugh as she moved into the tiny kitchen. "I've already been into it, to be honest. I just poured my second glass."

It didn't seem right—Hunter felt as though he knew Melanie so well, yet here he was seeing where she lived for the very first time. She had dish towels with apples on them, which struck him as odd. He wouldn't have pegged her as a kitschy kitchen kind of girl.

The hell with this tiptoeing-around-each-other crap. Hunter had touched and tasted every single inch of her. She stood with her back to him and he slid in behind her, lifting her hair to kiss the back of her neck. She jumped with such a jerk her wineglass skittered across the countertop and spilled.

"Damn!" she said, still not looking at him as she scooted past to tear a paper towel off the roll and mop up the mess.

"I'm sorry," he said, shoving his hands into his pockets. He was still wearing his coat over his jeans and thermal shirt, and he peeled the outer layer off and tossed it on the back of a chair, needing something to do. He felt restless. "How has work been?"

"Fine." She finally stopped fussing and turned to hand him a glass of wine. "You?"

They were doing this. The whole polite conversation crap. Like two total strangers. "It's a job," he said with a shrug. "Now come here, Melly."

"What?" she asked, flustered. The wineglass was between them like a shield.

"What do you mean, what?" The question irritated him. "I want a kiss."

"Oh." Her cheeks turned pink.

She was wearing a tight sweater in an oatmeal color, but the neck was so damn high he'd never achieve any access to her skin by going that route. So he decided to approach from below. Taking the glass out of her hand, he tossed half his wine back with one swallow before setting it aside and advancing on her until she bumped up against the counter. He thought she would reach for him, but she didn't. If anything, she had the look of hunted prey. It instantly killed his arousal.

"What's wrong?" he asked her, his voice sounding gruffer than he intended. He was on uneven ground here, not sure how to proceed. He'd never taken an affair to the dating stage before. Hell, he'd never had an affair. He'd had a couple of one-night stands, and then three fairly serious relationships. This was uncharted territory, and frankly, he wasn't enjoying it.

"Nothing is wrong," she whispered. For the first time, she actually looked him in the eye. "I'm just embarrassed."

Again, not a promising beginning to the evening. "About what?"

"I don't know."

Helpful. This was exactly what he had been afraid of. "Is there something you need to tell me, or talk about? You can tell me anything, you know that."

There it was. He heard it. He'd gone right back into the role of counselor.

"It's just that I don't feel as though I should talk to you about Ian."

No. No, she shouldn't. Because he really didn't want to hear it. Yet if she needed to talk, how could he tell her no? "Whatever is on your mind."

Melanie poured herself a new glass of wine to replace what had been spilled. She sipped it and appeared to weigh her words. "I told him I slept with you. I know it was inappropriate, and I shouldn't have done that without letting you know but…"

Hunter's stomach clenched. "But you wanted to hurt him. Or at least let him know that you weren't sitting around crying." It was a natural response; he understood that. But it confirmed what he'd been afraid of—that she wasn't in any position to be starting a new relationship. Not yet. Melanie needed time to process what had happened with Ian and to heal. Just because she hadn't loved him didn't mean she didn't have emotions she needed to put to bed.

"I did, which is petty."

It had also put Hunter's job in jeopardy, but he wasn't going to point that out. Melanie looked miserable enough as it was. He wasn't going to add to her burden. Which meant that he was going to retreat on this whole dating thing. She wasn't ready for this. Hell, he wasn't ready for this. He was too damn worried he was going to hurt her. Not to mention he couldn't stand there like an idiot and listen to her talk about her ex when she hadn't even kissed him yet.

For the past five days he'd thought of almost nothing but Melanie, wishing he could see her. And now that he was here with her, she didn't seem concerned with anything other than the fact that she'd blabbed about their fling. This was exactly why he'd wanted to keep it contained in Cancún.

"I think it's normal," he told her, taking the glass from her hand and setting it on the counter. "You spent a year with him. He hurt you."

Knowing what he had to do, Hunter leaned forward, cupping her cheeks. He searched her face, wanting to memorize it, wanting to remember every moment of their time together, as short as it had been.

"Why are you looking at me like that?" she whispered.

Instead of answering, he covered her mouth with his, taking her lips softly and giving her the deepest, most sensual kiss he knew how to give. He wanted it to tell her everything. That he thought she was amazing. That he thought she was beautiful. Extraordinary. Generous. Sexy. He wanted her to know that she had brought a positive energy and happiness to his life that he hadn't even known was missing.

"I'm not looking, I'm tasting," he said, pulling her earlobe gently between his teeth.

"Why does this feel like a goodbye kiss?" Melanie asked, drawing away from him and shooting him a suspicious look.

His throat felt tight, but he gave a slow nod. "I guess you could call it that. Or how about a postponed-for-now kiss?"

"What the hell does that mean?"

Hunter took a step away from her. "It means that you're not ready to do this. *We're* not ready to do this. I can't be the lover who walks you through your breakup. I just can't. It's only going to have me repeating the same damn mistakes I made with Danielle."

"This has nothing to do with Ian or Danielle," she said, her hands gripping the countertop behind her, knuckles white. "What are you afraid of?"

"Of hurting you. I've told you that all along."

"You're hurting me right now."

That sliced him a little, but he knew he was right. "Better now than later. Give me a call when you feel as though you're over Ian. When you've really let go."

For a second she looked stunned, her chest rising and falling with her rapid breathing. Then she narrowed her eyes. "I have let go. It's you who hasn't."

He had no idea what she meant by that. "I don't have anything to let go of."

"Bullshit. Just go, Hunter. Leave. Walk away, like Ian. It seems to be really easy."

Now he was angry in return. "That's not fair."

"Fair?" Her voice rose. "Are you kidding me? You know what, you're right. I broke the rules. I asked for more when you told me right from day one that I was never going to be more than a vacation romp to you."

She knew she was lashing out, but it still infuriated him to the point that his nostrils were flaring, and he was clenching and unclenching his fists. He wasn't going to engage with her. He wasn't going to sling barbs back.

"Call me sometime, Melly." Hunter yanked his coat off the back of the chair and headed back down the hallway.

"I'll give you credit," she said from behind him. "At least you had the balls to dump me in person instead of in a note."

For a second he paused, wanting to explain to her until she understood, but he knew enough to know that it would only make it worse.

So instead he opened the door and left, that pit in his gut growing more cavernous by the second.

15

"I STILL CAN'T believe you shagged the bodyguard," Ian said for the seven thousandth time. "Or that you felt the need to tell me."

Melanie rubbed her forehead, a headache stabbing her behind the eyes. "Do we have to go over this again? I only came into your office to discuss your travel schedule for next month."

A week solid this had been going on, and she was exhausted. She wasn't sleeping. She wasn't eating. She was forcing herself into the office every day and listening to Ian lament her apparent poor taste in moving on after he had dumped her.

Part of her had wanted to shame Ian for his thoughtless actions, and that had partially motivated her blurting out the truth. He didn't seem to get that you couldn't hurt and embarrass someone then act as though none of it had ever happened. When she had returned to work, he had done precisely that, and she had wanted to make him feel *something*. So she had blabbed. It had been a regrettable error in judgment because he couldn't seem to let it rest.

Now she was standing in front of him while he lounged behind his desk, swiveling in his chair. She gripped the file folder containing the hard copies of his schedule she had been attempting to show him.

"But we just broke up," Ian said. "I didn't expect you would jump the bodyguard five minutes later."

It had been a good twelve hours later, she would have him know. Actually, she would not have him know that. It was really none of his business. She was offended that somehow he seemed to think poorly of her behavior, yet his apology for his had been half-assed at best. And come to think of it, why did he assume that she had thrown herself at Hunter?

"Ian, you lied to me. You set me up for complete humiliation by putting me on a plane thinking that you and I were still going to have our romantic getaway—which *I* paid for—albeit a little later in the day. Then this total stranger you've stuck me with hands me a note with no vows of love in it, no apologies, just a cut-and-dried 'it's over.' So I think that under the circumstances it's incredibly arrogant of you to judge me for what I did." Melanie was starting to get worked up as she remembered that awful moment on the plane.

"Well. Apparently, he was a good shag."

Oh, no, he didn't. She prayed for patience. Or a modicum of restraint. But she was pretty sure she had neither. She was still reeling from the fact that Hunter had exited her apartment so unceremoniously. As if it didn't matter. As if she didn't matter. But Hunter wasn't in front of her, Ian was, and she'd about had it with men in general.

"That's irrelevant! The whole point is that you hurt me tremendously. I was mortified. If Hunter hadn't been there I would have spent the entire week lying on a beach chair crying. I would have canceled all my excursions and felt sorry for myself, drinking margaritas solo in the most pathetic waste of my hard-earned money ever. Fortunately, Hunter was there to keep me company."

"You don't have to brag about it. I get it—you had sex with the hot guy."

Wow, was this man thick. Had he always been like this?

Probably.

Ian continued, "I texted you. If you had responded I would have flown down and joined you. I realized my mistake almost immediately."

"I don't have an international data plan." It seemed as if he should know that about her. It seemed as if they both should have known a lot of things.

"That's not my problem, is it?"

Maybe not. Melanie sighed, her shoulders relaxing. She was angry with Ian for the way he had treated her, but she was also angry with herself for the way she had *allowed* him to treat her. Was he really behaving any different than he had during their relationship? Not really. So while she could blame him, she also had to accept responsibility for her part.

"Ian, it's funny to me that for a photographer, you don't see people very clearly."

"What is that supposed to mean?" Ian wrinkled his nose, making his glasses slip.

Melanie thought about the picture Hunter had taken when they were in the hammock. "You don't *see* me." Hunter saw her. He had her in his focus all the time. In a deep focus.

It hit her with stunning clarity how true that was. Yet she hadn't had him in the same focus. She had done precisely what he said Danielle had done. She'd leaned on him and offered to listen, but hadn't actually done it.

She was a fool for not just opening her mouth and telling him at the airport how she felt, for agreeing with him that, yes, she needed time to figure her stuff out but not insisting that she was absolutely sure about one thing—she wanted Hunter. Staring at Ian, she felt nothing but empathy for him and his self-absorption. There was no point in regrets. She may have spent a year with him, but she had learned a number of valuable lessons, and it wasn't wasted time for that reason.

"I have no idea what you're talking about. I'm looking right at you. I've shot you before. I see and appreciate the line of your neck and the slightly crooked smile you have. Your hair is a fantastic color when fading sunlight hits it."

Yeah. Ian didn't get it. He might never understand. Maybe his photographer's eyes were too trained to see her body and its reaction to his lens, instead of her soul.

"Ian." Feeling her throat tighten up, Melanie leaned forward and dropped the file. "Thank you for everything. I'm turning in my resignation."

"You're quitting your job? This is ludicrous. Why the hell do you need to quit? I need you, Melanie."

Which was precisely why she was quitting. She wanted to be wanted, not needed. "It's time. I've outgrown the position."

She had. God, it felt liberating to say that. Endorphins flooded her, and her cheeks went hot. Maybe quitting her job without a new one lined up was a dumb move, but she couldn't keep returning to the office day after day, subject to Ian's constant grilling and disappointment, her life on an endless loop with no progress. There was no reason to do that. Hunter was right. She needed a new job.

This was letting go. This was releasing all the constraints and expectations and fears from her life.

As she gave Ian a wave, she spun on her heel and marched out of his office.

She could feel herself grinning like an idiot, and several of her coworkers eyeballed her with suspicion. That was Ian handled. Job dealt with. Now she needed to talk to Hunter. No more tidy, efficient Melanie. She was Melly, and she was going to get messy and go after what she wanted. That lame-ass conversation she and Hunter had had wasn't good enough. It had been full of excuses, when really she'd been nervously trying to figure out how to tell him she was falling in love with him. They hadn't said everything that needed to be said, not by a long shot.

Her phone buzzed. It was a text from Ian. God, the man wouldn't stop.

I may have gotten the bodyguard fired.

Oh, dear God. No. No, no and no.

This was all her fault for opening her mouth to the wrong man. Instead of telling Hunter how she felt, she had revealed way too much information to Ian.

Feeling like an actor in a Christmas commercial or the star in a romantic comedy, Melanie fast walked in the direction of her cubicle, texting Hunter as she went. As soon as she hit Send, she realized that was stupid—she should call him, for crying out loud. Words on the screen could never have the impact of her voice telling him exactly what she needed to say: she was sorry she had gotten him fired, and she was in love with him.

She anxiously waited for him to pick up as she reached her desk, but he didn't. Staring at the screen didn't make him answer her text, either.

Melanie's life was heading in a direction that had no signs or maps to indicate whether she was on the right path. Letting go was terrifying and new. Determined to stay the course, she started packing some of her belongings, glancing at her phone approximately every five seconds.

HUNTER STARED AT his mother across the table and gave her an incredulous look. Since his plans for the next, oh, rest of his life, had disintegrated, he'd thought maybe he would feel slightly less like an ass if he took his mother out to dinner Friday night. But she was alternating between grilling him and doling out unwanted advice.

"I mean, honestly, I never really liked Danielle. I don't get why you're still moping over her." Sharon Ryan took a sip of her beer.

Wearing a deep V-neck sweater that could not be sufficient for retaining heat in these December temperatures, she had already attracted the attention of several older guys hanging out at the bar. Hunter was used to it. His sassy mother had always been a man magnet. It didn't make him any less freaked out, but he was used to it. The teen years had been filled with lots of shoving of his friends when they made "your mom" comments.

"Mom, Danielle hurt my ego, that's true. Mostly I was just disappointed that I wasn't going to have some company here at home after nine months in a sandbox. But I'm over it. It's all good." He was. It was the truth, just as he'd told Melanie, that it had been his ego that had been injured, not his heart. "This isn't about Danielle."

It was about Melanie.

It was about his own stupid inability to stay detached. He'd fallen for her like the proverbial ton of bricks. Only he hadn't told her. In retrospect, maybe that was a good thing, because it would have embroiled them in an emotional mess.

"Then for heaven's sake, what is it about? You look as though someone kicked your dog." Before he could respond she continued, "Is this about work? Your arm? It's okay to admit you're in pain."

"How do you know it's about anything? Maybe I'm just tired."

"Pfft." She rolled her eyes. "What are you, eighty? You're not tired. I know you—you brood. Have since you were little. It always meant one of two things—you were upset or you had to go to the bathroom."

Lord. Hunter reminded himself that he loved his mother. He really did. She was a tough lady, and the reason he was a fully functioning adult. For the most part anyway. But at the moment he was regretting the cruel irony of thinking she would serve as a distraction from his feelings about Melanie. Because now she was both embarrassing and bugging him. The only way to get her to back off was to just come clean and tell her the truth.

"Fine. I had sex with the client I was protecting in Cancún. More than once."

Her eyebrows shot up. "Oh. Did you get fired?"

"Yes, as a matter of fact, I did." That had been the final blow in a thoroughly shitty week. He wasn't angry with Melanie, though he would have appreciated some discretion. Mostly he was angry with himself. He needed this job. Yet he'd jumped in, balls to the wall, without even considering the consequences of an affair. Well, to be honest, he'd considered them, but it hadn't stopped him.

"Oh, damn, that sucks. I hope she did, at least—suck, that is."

Good God. "Mom." He reached for his own beer.

"What? Who wouldn't want that? I mean, what guy wouldn't?"

That actually made him laugh. "You're not right, you know that? You're not supposed to say things like that in front of your son."

"If not you, who?" She was shrugging and smiling. "Sorry, honey, it's too late for me to change now."

"I wouldn't want you to change." He wouldn't. Sharon was Sharon, and he loved her. "Okay, here's the deal. Melanie got dumped by her boyfriend as we were going down to Cancún. He was supposed to be there with her for a romantic week in Mexico, but instead he gave me a breakup note to give her after the door to the plane closed."

"What? Prick" was his mother's scathing opinion.

"Agreed. So she was all busted up over it, and we hit it off, and one thing led to another and, well, there you have it. What I wasn't expecting was to really like her, but I do. We had plans to get together this weekend, but then *she* was weird, and *it* was weird, and she told her ex, who is her boss, that we slept together, and I got fired."

"Holy hell, she was doing her boss and then she did the bodyguard? I like her style."

He frowned. "Mom. You're being inappropriate again."

She threw her hands up. "You're the one telling me you banged a client! How am I being inappropriate?"

Well. When she put it like that. "Fair enough. I just felt so bad that her boyfriend dumped her in a note." It stuck in his craw all over again saying it out loud.

"So it was like sympathy sex?"

"What? No, of course not!" This was going from bad to worse. "No, I mean at first, we were just offering each other comfort, yes, but I was attracted to her, and then I got to know her and I really liked her. Like her. She was great company, despite the fact that her boyfriend had blindsided her."

"I'm pretty sure I would have gotten on the next plane home and let the air out of his tires if my boyfriend did that to me."

"Oh, I have no doubt that's exactly what you would have done." His mom was very black-and-white on things like that.

"But I'm impulsive and a hothead, and that isn't always a good thing. So okay, you got fired and you yelled at her or something? Or she got home and got back with the ex?"

"No, I told her we shouldn't see each other. Before I got fired."

"What the hell is your problem?"

"I didn't want her to make a mistake on the rebound."

The minute he told her that, he knew what was coming.

"Oh, so you think being with *my* son would be a mistake?"

Yeah, that was exactly what he was expecting her to say. "Your son is sitting right in front of you, and I think that dating *anyone* on the rebound is a bad idea, but in particular, me. It didn't seem appropriate to butt in to her business."

"Oh, I think you already butted in to her business plenty, if you know what I mean."

He did. Hunter picked up one of his French fries and crammed it into his mouth so he wouldn't regress to being a defensive and bratty kid on her.

"I haven't had a successful relationship, in case you hadn't noticed. We had a good time. End of story."

"Which is why you're sitting across from me looking as though I grounded you on prom night. Do you want to see her?"

It was too hard to lie to his mother. She saw right through him. "Well, yeah, but…"

"But nothing. I didn't raise a quitter."

Hunter tossed down the other half of the fry, abandoning it. He had a sour taste in his mouth as he swallowed. "What the hell was I supposed to do?"

"Um, you tell her you want to make her forget all about her loser ex."

She was giving him a headache and making him feel seriously emasculated. "Mom, that's antiquated. Melanie needed to make her own decision about what she wanted. I can't be all 'come here, woman.' That's not how guys act now."

"Bullcrap. You should have picked her up and carried her off."

"You've seen *An Officer and a Gentleman* too many times."

"If it worked for Richard Gere, it can work for you."

Oh, my God. "I'm telling you, that doesn't work."

"You don't know if you don't try. It would work with me."

That he didn't doubt. His mother was a little over the top, but she might have a point. Whether it had been in Melanie's best interest or not, he had quit the field. He had wanted her to take some time and come to the conclusion that she did in fact want to date him. Hell, maybe his mother was right. Maybe he should have gone all alpha male and staked his claim.

"She called me and left a message saying she wanted to talk."

"This is not a time for talking. This is a call to arms." His mother gave a fist pump. "Do you have real feelings for her? This isn't just about a piece of ass?"

The expression appalled him. "No, of course not! I'm pretty sure I'm in love with her." He was. Melly was the sweetest, most generous and unforgettable woman he had ever met.

Now his mother just looked smug. "It's about damn time. I was starting to think you had a block of ice in your chest where your heart was supposed to be. Not a single woman has ever been able to melt you, but now you're like a snowman in a hothouse. I love it."

"I'm glad my misery is amusing to you."

"Don't be melodramatic." She reached over and squeezed his hand. "I'm happy for you, you big oaf. I want to see you happy and in love and thinking about settling down, getting married. Having children. That's all."

That made him feel a little remorseful. He knew she had his best interests at heart. He didn't need to snark at his mother, even when she was being outrageous. "Thanks. I know that."

"Then put on your man pants and go tell her how you feel." His mother shook her head. "If I had a dime for every time a man kept his trap shut when he should have opened it, I'd have a condo in Naples, Florida, by now."

He couldn't argue with her. He wasn't known for throwing it all out there. "Naples would bore you," he told her. "Too many old people."

"Rich single men, though."

"Stop."

She laughed. "Okay, I'll quit teasing you. But, God, it's just so easy to do."

"You're warped."

"Is Melanie anything like me?"

"No. She is probably the total opposite of you." He gave his mother a grin. "There is no competing with you, so I went for the other end of the spectrum. Melanie is a little naive, very sweet, organized."

"You're right, that isn't anything like me." She stole one of his fries. "You know, I think that's why I didn't like Danielle. She was my younger twin, so we butted heads."

Hunter had never thought about it before, but he could see it. "That's terrifying."

She laughed. "Well, I can't wait to meet the new girl."

"You're pretty confident in my charms." He wasn't so sure.

"Of course I am. I raised you, for one. But you're also your father's son, and that man was smoking hot and charming as hell. I couldn't resist him. So this girl will be putty, I have no doubt."

It was flattering, he supposed, both to himself and to his father. Yet all so very awkward.

He flagged the passing waiter down. "Can we have the check, please?"

Time to go home and regroup.

"Just remember, WWRGD," his mother said.

Did he even want to ask? "What does that stand for?"

"What would Richard Gere do?"

Okay, that made him laugh. "You're a lunatic." He lifted his beer to his lips and took a sip.

"And you're an officer *and* a gentleman."

Hunter choked on his beer. No wonder he had a ridiculous sense of humor. He came by it honestly. "Thanks for the vote of confidence. I'll do my best not to let you down."

Or himself. He wanted Melanie.

WWRGD?

Damn.

MELANIE SPENT SUNDAY evening checking her phone repeatedly and poring over the online job listings. Strangely, she wasn't experiencing the blind panic that she would have expected. She had quit her job on impulse. She was single, by choice in the case of Ian, and not by choice in the case of Hunter. But if she had learned anything from the past year, it was that she couldn't force someone to feel more for her than they did.

Ian hadn't contacted her again after she had stormed out of his office. She was planning to go back in on Monday, inform her coworkers, collect the rest of her things and leave. It would be ludicrous to put in two weeks' notice because it would be impossibly uncomfortable all around, but she needed to transition her work to other employees.

Melanie padded into the kitchen and pulled the previous day's leftover Chinese takeout from the fridge, dumping some on a plate.

No, work and Ian were not bothering her. Not really.

It was Hunter that was bothering her.

How could he just walk away and not bother to answer her texts or phone call? Why hadn't he wanted to see her at all? It didn't ring true to her that he was trying to protect her from getting hurt. That was such a bullshit guy cop-out.

She put her plate in the microwave and slammed the door shut, mentally kicking herself. The real reason was probably because she'd gotten him fired.

Dressed in the same pajamas she'd been wearing since Friday night, she bit her fingernails. She had to call him again. No texts. Gather her nerve and just do it.

Like the zip line. Just close her eyes and go.

She picked up her phone. It buzzed.

Nerves on edge, she jumped. "Oh, my God," she blurted out loud to her empty apartment. It was Hunter.

Can I pick you up at work tomorrow? We need to talk.

I don't think that's a good idea.

Her heart was hammering in her chest. He wanted to talk to her. That was good. That had to be good. Then she realized her response sounded totally wrong. Like she was suggesting talking was a bad idea. "What is wrong with me?" she groaned. "I can't be trusted to text."

I mean, maybe we can meet somewhere else? I'd love to talk. But maybe at work would be awkward?

She didn't exactly sound confident. But she was just so glad to hear from Hunter that she was typing faster than she was thinking. Or something like that. Why couldn't anyone just pick up the phone and call anymore? She could explain herself better. Faster.

I talked to Ian.

See, that was why texting was lame.

About what?

Melanie took a deep breath. She had to let him know everything. All of it. If he wanted to do this via text message, then so be it.

I quit my job. I don't want to work for Ian. I want a fresh start, somewhere I'll be appreciated.

After taking her food out of the microwave, she grabbed her fork and nervously shoveled a pile of noodles into her mouth.

You definitely deserve to be appreciated.

Okay, what did that mean? This was crazy.

He told me you got fired. I am so, so sorry, Hunter.

Melanie picked up the phone and hit Call on Hunter's contact page. She swallowed the lump of noodles caught in her throat.

"Hello?"

"I can't do texting," she said without a greeting, her voice sounding as if she'd been jogging for at least fifteen miles. Uphill. "I screw it up and everything sounds wrong. I'm really sorry about getting you fired. I should have kept my damn mouth shut, and I totally understand if you despise me."

"It's okay. I know you didn't mean for that to happen. I shouldn't have walked out the way I did." In return, he sounded gruff, like the Hunter she had first met. "That was a dick move."

"It wasn't what I wanted," she admitted. "It seemed so…abrupt."

She squeezed her eyes shut, wishing she knew what he was thinking.

A phone call was better than a text, but it was nothing like being in person, where you could see someone's expression. Touch him. This was so hard. She wanted to tell Hunter she had fallen in love with him, but she just couldn't do it over the phone. It wasn't right. She needed to read his reaction, see his eyes.

"I didn't mean to hurt you," he said.

And? He must have more to say than that.

There was a huge and grossly awkward pause.

Heat rose in her face, and she didn't know what to say. "Okay. Thank you."

They were back to the politeness they had been

displaying at her apartment. Where was the easiness they'd shared in Cancún?

"Are you okay?" he asked, sounding hesitant.

A phone call wasn't solving anything. Melanie felt the lump rise in her throat again. "Do you still want to get together tomorrow? Maybe we can meet somewhere convenient for both of us."

"Are you going to Bainbridge Studios?"

"Yes, I have to formally turn in my resignation and get some things from my desk."

"Will Ian be there?"

"I have no idea, but probably not. He has some appointments scheduled." She honestly did not understand what Hunter was getting at. He hadn't been this hard to interpret in Cancún. In fact, he had been pretty straightforward.

All week she had been hoping to hear from him, and now it wasn't helping to alleviate any of her fears or confusion.

She just felt…sad.

As though she had lost Hunter before she'd ever even had him.

"Hmm. Okay. Well, why don't you call me when you're done, and we can make some plans?"

That was a brush-off.

It meant by the time they talked and made plans they might end up meeting for coffee or a drink by eight at the earliest. After a week of wanting to see him and letting her nerves get the best of her, she was going to either blurt out her feelings in one embarrassing verbal vomit, or she was going to clam up completely.

She was already clamming up.

"Sure. Great. Have a good night," she said, as though she was ending a call with her accountant.

She had seen and touched every inch of Hunter. She had felt him moving inside her. But he felt as remote as the warm breeze and the sandy beach.

Her windows rattled from the howling winter wind.

Making a face at her plate, she tossed down her fork.

Her phone buzzed, and she picked it up, heart rate kicking up in anticipation. It was an alert on her calendar going off, telling her it was the longest night of the year.

Because she needed a reminder? Thanks, smartphone. She was already quite aware of that, thank you very much.

16

HUNTER HAD MEANT it when he'd told Melanie he wasn't great at voicing his emotions, nor was he was known for being particularly romantic. He thought that was pretty evident in how he'd handled everything since they'd gotten home from Cancún. He'd pretty much sucked hard at his delivery. His expertise was listening, not speaking.

Her phone call had reminded him that text messages were lame, and he was so annoyed at himself for not picking up the phone first, forcing her to do it, that he had been stiff throughout their conversation. For a minute there, he had actually thought maybe his mother was wrong, and it didn't matter one bit how much he cared about Melanie. She deserved better. But then he realized that the ultimate insult was not allowing her to make that choice for herself. If he respected and appreciated her, he should give her the opportunity to accept or reject him.

If she thought she was ready to date again after Ian, who the hell was he to say she wasn't? It was his role to offer support, not tell her what to do. It was his goddamn forte. He should have gone with his strength instead of running from it.

Blowing on his hands to warm them up, he stood outside her glass-front office building. No one had bothered to close the blinds, and with it getting dark so early, everyone inside was clearly visible through the windows. He could see Melanie packing up her desk, occasionally talking to various other employees who came by to speak to her. She was wearing a sweater, tight black pants and boots that came to her knees. Those boots were distracting as hell; they'd look great with a bra and panties and nothing else.

The image warmed him up from the inside out, that was for damn sure.

He was pacing back and forth like a voyeur, waiting for the right moment. Trouble was, he wasn't exactly sure what that moment would look like, and he figured he only had about ten more minutes before she finished up and walked out. He couldn't screw this up.

WWRGD?

His mother's voice popped into his head.

Crap.

He strode across the street and yanked open the door to Bainbridge Studios.

The receptionist looked up at him. "Oh, hello. Aren't you Mr. Ryan, from the security firm?"

"Yes."

He moved past her desk, ignoring the way the woman half stood up, startled. "You can't go in there…"

Hunter didn't care. He ignored all the stares as he moved across the open-concept office space, past several desks. He was going to unstick his tongue from the roof of his mouth and express his goddamn feelings if it killed him. A bullet would probably be easier to take.

Melanie turned suddenly, her eyes wide, as if she'd

sensed his presence. "Hunter?" she murmured, her voice sexy and low and filled with promise.

It reminded him of how she had sounded in bed, groaning his name into his ear as he'd buried himself deep inside her. How tender she had been, generous, quick to touch him, to cuddle. The beautiful way she had smiled at him in the hammock, captured on his phone in a shot he had spent an insane amount of time studying over the past two days.

"I thought you said to text you," she faltered.

He stalked right up to her, cupped her cheeks and kissed her for all to see. Her mouth trembled beneath his, and he kissed her hard, letting his lips speak the words he never had.

When he pulled back and saw that her eyes were filled with confusion, but also something more than that, he found the words.

"Melly, I've fallen in love with you. I know that sounds crazy, but I don't want to just see you casually or let things fizzle out because I didn't have the balls to tell you how I feel. Or because I'm afraid to hurt you, or I'm afraid you're going to hurt me. I want to be with you because I think you're amazing and beautiful and kind. I love you."

Melanie stared up at Hunter in shock. He loved her. He. Loved. Her.

It seemed impossible. But there was no doubting it because he'd said it, and Hunter never said anything he didn't mean. He also didn't like to throw everything all out there in front of other people, yet he had.

He looked so gorgeous in his suit, all strong jaw and intense eyes. She smoothed his tie down over his chest, feeling suddenly very overwhelmed and tender toward him. "I love you, too. I've been wanting to tell you that for a few days, but I thought you'd think that I'd lost my mind."

"You haven't lost anything. You've gained a man. Whether you like it or not."

Shivers rolled up her spine like a convoy of electricity. A man. Not a convenient and sensible relationship, but a man.

"Oh, I like it." She yanked his tie harder. "I like it a lot."

"Let's get out of here, then." Hunter bent over and scooped her up into his arms.

Melanie gave an involuntary squeak of shock and embarrassment. All her coworkers were gawking at them. But then she realized she didn't care. She no longer wanted to hide.

"You always have the best ideas," she told him, wrapping her arms around his neck.

Her coworker Janice grabbed Melanie's purse and her coat off her desk and thrust them at her, her eyes wide with surprise and possibly a touch of envy.

"Thanks," Melanie said. The rest of her stuff could wait until tomorrow. Or never. She didn't particularly care about her stapler.

Hunter carried her across the office. "Dinner?" he asked.

"As long as it's delivery. My place is right around the corner." She had missed him. She didn't want to stare at him across a table in a restaurant—she wanted to be able to touch him. Repeatedly. In both mushy gushy ways, and in ways that were not appropriate for public viewing. Or even for a beach in Cancún.

"Delivery is fine with me. Let's consciously couple."

Melanie laughed. "You did not just say that."

Hunter shoved open the front door and grinned at her. "I did say that. You want me to show you what I mean?"

There was that shiver again, and it didn't have a damn thing to do with the blast of cold air that hit her in the face when they stepped outside. "Yes."

So he did. Until Melanie forgot what *conscious* meant, but was well aware of the definition of *couple*.

* * * * *

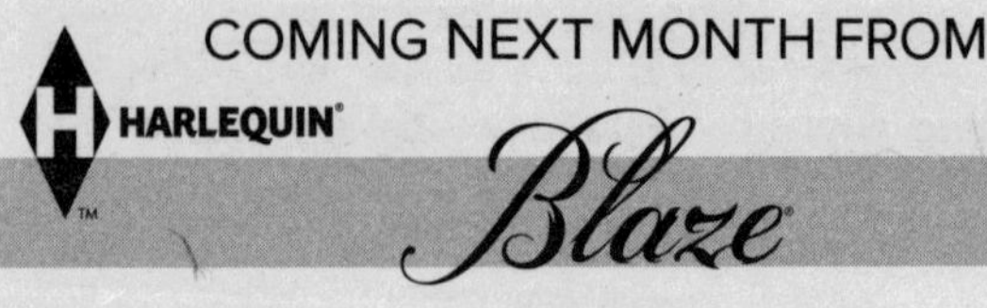

Available April 21, 2015

#843 A SEAL'S PLEASURE

Uniformly Hot!

by Tawny Weber

Tessa Monroe is used to men falling at her feet, but Gabriel Thorne is the first one to kiss his way back up to her heart. Can this SEAL's pleasure last, or will their fling end in tears?

#844 INTRIGUE ME

It's Trading Men!

by Jo Leigh

Lisa Cassidy is a PI with a past and Daniel McCabe is the sexy doc she's investigating. But everything changes after an unexpected and sizzling one-night stand...

#845 THE HOTTEST TICKET IN TOWN

The Wrong Bed

by Kimberly Van Meter

Laci McCall needs to lie low for a while so she goes home to Kentucky. She doesn't expect to end up in bed with Kane Dalton—her first love and the man who broke her heart.

#846 OUTRAGEOUSLY YOURS

by Susanna Carr

To revamp her reputation, Claire Miller pretends to have a passionate affair with notorious bachelor Jason Strong. But when their fling becomes a steamy reality, Claire can't tell what's true and what is only fantasy.

SPECIAL EXCERPT FROM

Look for more sexy SEAL stories in the ***UNIFORMLY HOT!*** *miniseries!*

Read on for a sneak preview of
A SEAL'S PLEASURE
by New York Times *bestselling author*
Tawny Weber.

Tessa Monroe looked at the group of men who'd just walked in.

Her heart raced and emotions spun through her, too fast to identify.

"Why is he… Are they here?" she asked her friend Livi.

"The team? You don't think Mitch would celebrate our engagement without his SEALs, do you?" Livi asked as she waved them over.

As one, the men looked their way.

But Tessa only saw one man.

Taller than the rest, his shoulders broad and tempting beneath a sport coat the same vivid black as his eyes, he managed to look perfectly elegant.

His gaze locked on her, sending a zing of desire through her body with the same intensity as it had the first time he'd looked her way months before.

Tessa Monroe, the woman who always came out on top when it came to the opposite sex, wanted to hide.

"That's so sweet of his friends to come all this way to celebrate your engagement," she said, watching Livi's fiancé stride through the crowd to greet the group.

HBEXP0415

“They’re all based in Coronado now. Didn’t I tell you?” Livi asked, her eyes locked on Mitch as if she could eat him up. “Romeo’s the best man.”

Romeo.

Tessa’s smile dropped away as dread and something else curled low in her belly.

Gabriel Thorne. Aka, Romeo.

His eyes were still locked on her and Tessa could see the heat in that midnight gaze.

It was as if he could look inside her mind, deep into her soul—and see everything. All of her desires, her every need, her secret wants.

A wicked smile angled over his chiseled face, assuring her he not only saw them all, but that he was also quite sure that he could fulfill every single one. And in ways that would leave her panting, sweaty and begging for more.

There was very little Tessa didn’t know about sex. She appreciated the act, reveled in the results and had long ago mastered the ins and outs of, well, in and out. She knew how to use sex, how to enjoy sex and how to avoid sex.

So if anyone had told her that she’d feel a low, needy promise of an orgasm curling tight in her belly from just a single look across a crowded room, she’d have laughed at them.

Love the Harlequin book you just read?

Your opinion matters.

Review this book on your favorite book site, review site, blog or your own social media properties and share your opinion with other readers!

JUST CAN'T GET ENOUGH?

Join our social communities
and talk to us online.

You will have access to the latest news on upcoming titles and special promotions, but most importantly, you can talk to other fans about your favorite Harlequin reads.

Harlequin.com/Community

Facebook.com/HarlequinBooks

Twitter.com/HarlequinBooks

Pinterest.com/HarlequinBooks